Both creatures had been hurt but could still move. In a reaction of either reflex or panic, the larger one had immediately begun to turn away from the direction of the cyborg's attack.

The cyborg got off two more grenades, seconds apart, and both of the monsters were literally blown in two by the followup shots. They were immobile now, their rear sections lying inert except for the convulsive thrashing of their remaining legs. The tentacles extending from the fronts of their bodies were flailing wildly, beating the ground and whipping through the air.

The cyborg lowered his arms again, locked his wrists so that his palms were facing outward, and pointed both extremities at the monsters again. The stuff that comprised the insides of their bodies began to break up and flow across the road. It looked as if the things were being shaken apart, invisibly reduced to their smallest components. . . .

CYBORG COMMANDO™

BOOK 1

PLANET IN PERIL

by Pamela O'Neill and Kim Mohan

Cover illustration by Janny Wurts

PLANET IN PERIL

A CYBORG COMMANDO™ Book

First printing, December 1987
Printed in the United States of America

Distributed by the Berkley Publishing Group, 200 Madison Ave-
nue, New York NY 10016

9 8 7 6 5 4 3 2 1

ISBN: 0-441-66883-6

New Infinities Productions, Inc.
P.O. Box 127
Lake Geneva WI 53147

For our children . . .

John, Marc, Katie, Megan, and Ryan

. . . who were with us every word of the way

Prologue

It was out there from the start. Then the sun was but a formless, inert lump of matter.

It was out there when life began in the warm, sunlit shallow ponds near the coasts of the newly formed seas.

It started to take notice when animal life first appeared in the water and It watched as single-celled organism evolved to insect, to fish, to reptile, to mammal, and then finally to bipedal, consciously motivated human being.

It began to pay close attention when science emerged from medieval darkness and man embarked on his faltering ascent to the stars. It noted that of all of the lower life forms, man seemed to fear the insect most of all.

It would remember that.

It saw one man take one small step that was applauded by all mankind. And It later watched as seven members of that species, in trying to soar toward new heights, instead plummeted to their deaths as the result of some other human's error.

It grew arrogant as time went on. Using man's terminology, It "laughed" when man began to speculate about the possibility of being visited by "other" intelligent life forms. That this inferior representation of a thinking organism considered itself intelligent was Its favorite joke.

It waited and It watched, with an obsession even It would have been hard pressed to explain. And finally, It had seen enough.

It came swiftly, without warning, and with a force so devastating that in the span of a few earthly days the assault almost destroyed everything man had spent thousands of years making.

Almost . . . .

For all of Its planning, for all of Its perfect timing, It made one potentially disastrous error — It underestimated the inhabitants of the planet Earth and what they would do to save their world.

1

January 13, 2035

Not once during the nineteen-plus years of Cris Holman's life had he seen a more spectacular sight. A niveous fantasy, hissing and roaring and dancing around the tiny vehicle that dared to disturb its symmetry and had the audacity to storm across its pure, white carpet, leaving ugly indentations wherever it went.

The wipers on the small, silver car slid rhythmically back and forth across the curved windshield, fruitlessly attempting to keep it clear of snow while the cold wind seemed to howl in delight as it enjoyed an edge in this tedious little game.

"Damn!" Cris cursed loudly as the laser cartridge sound system he'd installed less than a week ago abruptly stopped working for the third time in ten minutes. He gave the left door that housed one of the speakers a hard, angry rap with his fist and swore again, this time taking care to expel the bits of profanity in a brief, passionate diatribe on the shortcomings of so-called modern technology.

Cris sighed, reached out, and ejected the sound cartridge. What the hell, he thought in an attempt to rationalize. The way that wind's whistling, who needs music anyway? He tried to relax as he eased the car along the seemingly deserted highway. The vehicle glided along the ice-covered road, the back wheels occasionally swinging slightly to one side or the other as the front wheels fought to pull the car through the snow.

The daily drive from Whitewater, Wisconsin, to his family's Delavan Lake home was one that Cris normally made in about twenty-five minutes. During the storms of the last three days, however, each one-way trip had taken more than an hour.

Cris, like most Wisconsin natives, usually took the brutal winter weather in stride. In fact, he actually enjoyed this time of year because he could spend some of his free time on the snow-covered ski slopes at Alpine Valley, where he had worked as a downhill instructor for the past two years. But the conditions of the last few days had been worse than any Cris had seen before.

The southeast section of the state had been enjoying rather mild weather, even for January — until last Thursday. Then all hell broke loose, and not just in Wisconsin. An outburst of violent weather had the world in its grasp and seemed intent on not letting go.

Scientists attributed the drastic weather changes to a freak accident at a Chinese air-testing station near the South Pole. According to news accounts, the impact of a large meteorite had caused the detonation of about twenty nuclear devices hidden at the site. A rise in tides, brought about by the breakup and melting of trillions of tons of ice, was causing widespread damage to the world's seacoasts. Surface naval operations had become impossible, and air travel was nearly at a standstill in the areas that were beset by storms.

Most of the world was shocked to learn about the existence of the weapons. However, that emotion was soon overshadowed by bewilderment and terror as it became apparent that the aftereffects of the accident were doing much more damage than the explosion itself actually caused.

The only way in which all of this directly affected Cris's world was the extra amount of time it took him to drive to and from his classes at the University of Wisconsin-Whitewater. He had little interest in politics, and even less in meteorology — except when the weather forced him to change his plans or waste some of his precious free time.

Bad as it was, the turbulent weather had failed to keep him home on this particular Saturday, when he normally wouldn't have had to make the round trip. He had gone to Whitewater to see Maura — and, as he told his parents before leaving the house this morning, he would "gladly have driven through a hurricane" to be able to spend some extra time with her.

Cris chuckled to himself as he thought about how overdramatic a person in love could be. He smiled self-consciously, feeling a bit foolish about some of the things he often found himself saying when he was alone with Maura. But he couldn't suppress his feelings for her. To him, she was the most beautiful, most exciting woman in the world.

At first glance, there was nothing physically distinctive about Maura. Her five-foot, eight-inch frame was slim but well proportioned and exuded a very subtle sexuality that became more apparent — and more exciting — the longer you looked at her. Her black hair was gently streaked with silver highlights in the style of the day. She kept it closely cropped so that it attractively framed her pixieish face.

She and Cris had met four months ago, at the start of Cris's second year at the college. She was beginning graduate work there after having received her Bachelor of Science degree, majoring in biochemistry. He had seen her sitting alone in the student social center several times during the first few days of school. Then one day, while he was working out on the parallel bars in the gymnasium, he had noticed her out of the corner of his eye as she walked by a short distance away. The momentary distraction caused him to miss his timing and take a tumble onto the padded mat beneath him. Embarrassing as it was, the maneuver did attract her attention.

He smiled now, remembering how he had looked up at her and said, in his best impersonation of the classic comedian Pee-Wee Herman, "I meant to do that!" They both laughed, and the ice was broken.

The snow-covered ice on the pavement stretching before him at the moment, however, was another matter. "Oh, great! Now the sandblowers are frozen up!" Cris grumbled. In fact, the metal spouts at the side of the highway had stopped spitting sand a mile or two back, but he'd been too wrapped up in reminiscing to notice. "I'll be lucky to get home before dark at this rate."

Cris maneuvered the car through a gentle curve but stabbed at the brake a little too strongly, which caused the back end to begin sliding off the road. "Come on, baby," he coaxed as he turned the wheel slightly to the right in an effort to keep the car under control. After a few harrowing seconds, all four wheels grabbed the road once again.

At that instant Cris felt a contradictory combination of relief and gnawing anxiety, noting that the weather, which he had thought couldn't be much worse, seemed to be getting more severe. He let up on the accelerator, slowing the car to fifteen miles per hour. At this speed he was traveling more slowly than the wind, which was driving the snow in the same direction the car was moving. Snow squalls swirled past the vehicle with increasing frenzy. He could feel the car moving, but when he looked out the window it appeared as if he was stationary in the middle of a blizzard. Cris peered out the windshield and frowned. This is no way to end a perfect day, he thought. . . .

Cris had arrived at Maura's apartment at midmorning, expecting to accompany her to a stuffy luncheon to welcome a visiting scientist to the university. The man had been conducting a series of lectures at colleges across the country, and the Whitewater campus was one of his scheduled stops. He was a famous figure in the world of biochemistry and Maura, whose ambition was to become just as well known in that field, had been something just short of rapturous when she had received an invitation to attend the luncheon. She, in turn, had asked Cris to be her escort.

He had not been looking forward to being with Maura in the company of a lot of people with whom he had nothing in common. He'd much rather have spent the day inside, alone with her. He liked her apartment and was beginning to see it as a second home. An old architectural delight, the furnished dwelling had high ceilings, authentic oak trim, solid oak interior doors, and a huge, brick, wood-burning fireplace. The couple had spent many happy hours stretched in front of the warm fire. And although he didn't know it before he arrived there, the two were about to spend a few more of the same on this cold, blustery winter day.

When Maura opened the door of her apartment, Cris knew right away they would not be attending a luncheon. Maybe it was the short, silk robe that barely covered her shapely thighs and hung open in front, partially revealing her well-formed breasts. Or maybe it was the fact that she was barefoot and barelegged except for the thick copper ankle bracelet he had given her for Christmas. The sweet smell of burning pinewood drifting through the open doorway further aroused his suspicions. And the look in her eyes confirmed them.

"Hi there." Maura greeted a delighted Cris with a sweet, seductive smile, standing to one side so he could get in.

"Hello!" Cris grinned back, stepping inside and closing the door behind him.

It turned out that the guest of honor's plane had been grounded in Chicago because of the bad weather, and Cris was delighted. The next several hours were some of the best the young lovers had ever spent together. Cris hated to leave when the time came, but he had promised his younger sister Sara that he would drive back home in time to help her celebrate her seventh birthday. A family dinner was planned, and he was looking forward to the occasion almost as much as she was.

He thought about Sara now, and smiled with brotherly pride and love as he turned the car left onto the back road leading from the small village of Darien to the north shore of Delavan Lake. He hoped that when he had children some day, they would all have Sara's sweet disposition and perpetual enthusiasm.

Only about three miles to go. Cris doubted he would make the trip again for a couple of days, until he was sure the weather had calmed down a bit. But he intended to phone Maura later tonight, and probably at least a couple of times tomorrow. He got a big lump in his throat every time he thought about her.

He smiled inwardly, but the feeling abruptly turned to one of terror as he saw what appeared to be a large wall of snow and ice blocking the road ahead of him. He slammed on the brakes, knowing even as he did so that he wouldn't be able to stop in time. The car skidded sideways and hit the obstacle broadside. Just after the left side of the car hit the wall, Cris's head cracked hard against the driver's-side window.

That was the last sensation he felt until a few minutes later, when he came to and quickly determined that, except for a painful lump on his head, he wasn't hurt.

"What the hell?" he cried in bewilderment as he looked out over swirling snow and terrain that was again featureless. He remembered crashing into something — what, he wasn't quite sure — but now it was gone! He began to wonder if he had been hallucinating and had simply imagined an obstacle in front of him.

Still trying to clear his head, Cris reached forward and turned the starter key. The engine hummed to life, but when he gently pressed on the accelerator the front tires simply spun in place, and the car stayed where it was.

Cris shut off the car, rested his head against the back of the seat, and took a deep breath. He slowly unfastened his seat belt and pulled the door handle upward, but the latch was jammed. Fortunately, the passenger door opened normally.

As he climbed out of the car, his right foot abruptly plunged into about a foot of snow. "Wonderful!" he said sarcastically as he saw that the back half of the car was embedded in a snowbank at the side of the road. He fastened his insulated parka all the way up to his chin and pulled the hood tight around his face. He took his gloves out of his pocket and quickly covered his hands. Then he trudged toward the front of the car to check out the left side. The front fender and door were slightly crumpled. The car didn't appear to be very badly damaged, but it was obvious to Cris that he had indeed hit something with the left side of the vehicle — and the way the snow was packed around the back end, he wasn't going to be able to drive any farther for now.

"Guess I walk the rest of the way," he muttered, and walked back around the car, crawled in through the passenger side, and eased himself back into the driver's seat. He started the car again. Although he was almost certain it would be a useless effort, he pressed softly on the accelerator and tried to rock the car back and forth to free it from the snow. It was no use — the front tires couldn't get enough of a grip on the road to pull the back end out of the snow.

Cris turned off the engine and sighed. Then, after pulling his hood down around his face as far as he could without covering his eyes, he got out of the car and started following the road that led to his house.

"Sara had better appreciate this!" he muttered to himself, trying to keep his spirits up. "I could be sitting in front of a warm fireplace right now. Or better yet, I could be . . . ." He interrupted himself with a smile.

The sky, which was completely clouded over and had provided little light all day, began getting even darker as the evening hours approached. As Cris walked, he kept his eyes open for signs of life inside any of the few scattered homes he needed to pass before reaching his destination. But he didn't have much hope of finding anyone in them this time of year, since most of the houses in this area were only occupied in the summer.

The eerie sounds of winter filled the air around

him. Most of them he was familiar with — the crunching of snow beneath his feet, the soft impact of frozen snowflakes as they piled on top of one another, the howling of the wind, and his own, labored breathing. One sound, however, was not consistent with the rest of the winter scene. Once in a while, when the wind let up for a moment, Cris thought he heard a low rumbling sound, almost like continuous thunder, coming from the trees off to his right. He decided the accident had left him jittery and tried to ignore the strange noise. He did, however, begin to move more rapidly, since darkness was beginning to settle in around him. A little more than an hour and a half later he turned onto the winding, one-lane road that led to his house.

It wasn't until he rounded the last curve in the road that he spotted them. At first he thought he was seeing things.

It knew differently. They were real. And they weren't going to go away.

2

"Aw, come on. This might be the last chance I get to enjoy myself in the manner in which puberty forced me to become accustomed." John Edwards smiled his best boyish grin and rested back on the pillow, his hands behind his head — a perfect picture of feigned innocence.

"Sorry, Sergeant Edwards. My orders are to prep you for surgery. I haven't been told to prep you for anything else." Gina Miller gave her patient a condescending smile as she resolutely held out a handful of varicolored capsules.

"But you don't understand!" The young recruit sat bolt upright in bed, attempting to portray a combination of urgency and sincerity. He obligingly reached for the handful of pills, but instead of taking them held tightly onto the hand that offered them. "The only way I can gather the courage to go through with this brave deed is if you agree to be my last thrill in life. The way you look, I'm sure it will be enough to last me through the lifetime I will be forced to go without. Think of it as a contribution to all mankind." He leaned back on one elbow, the mischievous grin returning. "And it'll probably do you for eternity, too, if what I'm told about my bedside manner is true."

Gina shook her head and clucked her tongue in mock disgust. "And you're supposedly one of the finest examples the military has to offer? God help mankind!" She pulled her hand away, carefully making sure that the capsules were exchanged from nurse to patient in the process. She opened the door as if to leave, but halfway through turned and, in a seductive tone of voice, added, "If you're really looking for a good time, take those pills. They're just what the doctor ordered." She winked and left the room.

Sergeant John Edwards rolled his eyes and fell back on the bed, still clutching the medication. His palms were sweaty and his heart rate was greatly accelerated.

He was scared. And he had good reason to be.

He had volunteered for this assignment be-cause he believed in the Cyborg Commando pro-gram. Scientists had figured out how to build a better soldier, and John Edwards believed that the safety of the world and the eventual de-escalation of the nuclear tension that had hung over the head of mankind for nearly a century depended on the success of the program.

He had spent weeks studying all of the available information concerning the Cyborg Commando experiment before he had made up his mind to be a volunteer — to allow his brain to be transplanted into a mechanical body, while his own perfect (or so he saw it) specimen of flesh and bones waited in cryogenic storage.

Waited for what? John had often asked himself that question during the testing and briefing period preceding his actual acceptance into the program. John was told there was good reason to believe that the same group of scientists who had invented the Cyborg Commando technology would eventually be able to come up with a way to reunite body and brain. But for the moment, at least, the process was irreversible.

"Yeah, and by the time that happens, if it ever does, my poor brain will probably be tired and senile and my body frigid from years of being on ice," John had told the military doctor who had filled him in on the risks involved in the operation. The doctor had said nothing, nor had his expression indicated that he was amused by what the young recruit had to say.

The previous results of the experiment, though encouraging, included some failures that made

John Edwards's pending operation one of concern for all involved — especially for him. He had not learned any details about these failures from the members of the military briefing team — they simply said that there had been "some unsuccessful attempts during which a few brave men before you lost their lives." Of course, these "few brave men" were honored posthumously and their names were added to the roster of the hundreds of thousands of military men who had died in service to their country.

But there were rumors surrounding the deaths of these experimental soldiers that, if true, had to make what John Edwards was facing one of the most terrifying prospects he could imagine.

He had heard, and wanted not to believe, that a member of one of the medical teams involved in performing some of the experimental operations had resigned after two such supposed failures. According to this person, who had spoken in confidence (or so he had thought) to a few friends who were sitting around drinking one evening, the brains of two former human beings had gone through such shock and terror when disconnected from their bodies that, once they were hooked up to their new mechanical systems, they had screamed unceasingly until they were disconnected — for good — three days after the operations had been completed.

John shuddered. "You'd think I'd receive some

special treatment, considering the risks," he said loudly, in mock disgust, as he popped one of the eight pills into his mouth.

He tried to remember what the various drugs were for. He had been thoroughly briefed on everything that he would be going through from the beginning of the operation until the end of his one-week recovery period. After that, assuming he survived, a lot depended on his frame of mind. But it was hard, now that the moment was near, to care about seemingly minor details, such as which pill did what. He shrugged and chased the pill down his throat with a mouthful of water.

The only fact that mattered right now was that he had volunteered for this duty, and he was not the type to chicken out of anything. He could not turn back and manage to retain any pride. No, it went deeper than pride — he had always been big on self-respect, and John Edwards had a definite feeling that if he backed out now, he wouldn't be able to live with himself from then on. Life inside a mechanical body, such as it was, would be preferable to life inside a human body that didn't have the guts to go through with what he had promised to do.

The door of the military hospital room opened and an attractive woman entered.

"Oh, baby, I thought you'd never come!" John fawned overdramatically.

Nora Whitaker grinned knowingly. She'd spent a

lot of time with John in the last several weeks, and she was used to his verbal flirtations.

"I see you're in your usual mood," Nora teased, hoping to relieve some of the apprehension that she knew must lie beneath John Edwards's composed exterior.

"Oh, sir, you know it! And I can tell just by looking at you that you're just what the doctor would have ordered if he had known what sort of medicine I really need." The man who was soon to be Commando C-12 reached for the attractive woman who was seventeen years his senior.

Nora, as much as she liked this young man and as sympathetic as she felt toward him at the moment, was not the type of officer who would allow any breach of protocol, even under these circumstances. She gave Edwards a convincing military scowl. "Must I remind you, Sergeant Edwards, that I am your superior and, as such, you will take care how you address me?"

John smiled, defiance written all over his handsome face. "And what are you going to do if I don't — spank me, throw me out of the program, or both?"

"In recognition of the sacrifice you are about to make, I'll pretend I didn't hear that. But I warn you, sergeant — sacrifice or not, you are still a soldier and are subject to military discipline."

"Aw, shucks. I thought letting you turn me into a tin man would keep me off the court-martial list."

Nora grinned. There was no way not to like this young man. She admired his pluck and enjoyed his banter. She could not allow herself to show it, but she felt a little sad, selfishly, that he was among the ten new recruits awaiting the experimental procedure.

Nora Whitaker was a specialist presently attached to the United States Army, a psychologist by profession. She had previously worked with Richard Sawtell, the creator of the Cyborg Commando concept, in making his idea a reality. It was rumored that she had once been married, but she never talked about her personal life — past or present.

At thirty-eight years of age, Nora was an attractive woman whose face, nonetheless, was beginning to show some signs of wear. The thin lines around her eyes betrayed her age, which might otherwise have been hard to guess. Her honey-colored hair, though usually kept tightly contained in a severe knot at the nape of her neck, was breathtaking when it hung loose and free-flowing, measuring at least twenty inches from crown to tips. Her large, turquoise eyes, though somewhat reclusive and cold, sparkled almost hypnotically when she wanted them to.

Her nearly flawless complexion was probably her most striking feature; the skin on almost every part of her body looked like fine porcelain. Her tall, sinewy figure still resembled that of a much younger woman. Sergeant Edwards may have been teasing, but he wouldn't have turned down an opportunity to spend some quality time with the woman, even though she was almost twice his age.

"So tell me, young man," Nora began, emphasizing the fourth word, "how are you feeling this morning?"

"How am I *supposed* to feel? No one will let me do any touching!" Edwards retorted.

Nora smiled. She knew the jokes were an attempt to mask his fear. "Okay, you've had your fun. Now let's get down to business. Sergeant Edwards, I am obligated at this time to officially read you your rights of refusal, so—"

"Don't bother!" John snapped, briefly letting his real mood show through. "I know what you're going to say and I don't intend to back out, so spare me the speech!"

Nora gave him a moment to cool off before continuing. "I have to read this, John. You know that." Her tone was softer now, almost motherly.

"Okay," John said, his smile returning. "But can you strip while you do it? Then you won't be wasting my time."

Nora ignored his impertinence, looked back down at the paper she was holding and began to read. "Sergeant John David Edwards, it is my responsibility to inform you that the service you are about to perform, while one of utmost importance to the security of the free world, is also of a highly dangerous nature, with a success rate of only fifty percent as of this date and with, as yet, no known way to reverse the effects. Should you choose to go through with this operation, the outcome could be fatal.

"If the operation is a success you will, at best, be left with an entirely foreign body that will only outwardly resemble the one you now possess. You will not be able to continue enjoying many of the pleasures you have experienced in your organic body. You will, however, be free from the pain and physical suffering of normal-bodied men, and you will be superior to normal humans in many ways. All of these benefits are, of course, contingent upon you surviving the operation.

"The procedure you are about to undergo, should you still so choose, is a very difficult and time-consuming one — one during which you will remain aware, although for a time you will sense nothing to be aware of. You will, in essence, be trapped within your mind for a time, unable to communicate your feelings to anyone around you. You will feel no physical pain. However, the psychological effects have been known to render some volunteers mentally ill after the procedure. . . . At this point in time, do you have any questions?"

"No!" John shot the answer back without hesitating.

"Do you have any reservations?"

"No!"

"Sergeant Edwards, would you like to reconsider your decision to accept this assignment?"

"No!"

Official business out of the way, Nora Whitaker asked him a question of her own. "Are you scared, John?"

His eyes looked deep into the turquoise pools that stared down at him and, in the most serious tone of voice Sergeant John Edwards could ever remember using, he said, "Shitless."

3

January 13, 2035

Whatever they were, they were not of this world — of that Cris was certain.

He rubbed his eyes, although it was more of a reflexive movement than a functional one. Visibility was better here, since the trees tended to take a great deal of the snow and ice upon their branches. So Cris could see several hundred feet now, and no amount of eye-rubbing would remove the nightmarish scene in front of him.

The things reminded him of pictures he had seen of the tiny dust mite normally found in all households — but these were thousands of times larger and a million times more terrifying. And they were plodding around outside the home Cris shared with his family, trampling bushes and pushing their bodies against the exterior walls. Cris assumed that Sara and his parents were inside, since both of the family's vehicles — his father's truck and his mother's small car — were parked in the driveway, but the house was dark.

Cris squinted into the darkness, trying to get a better look at the things. Their insectlike forms, a sickening grayish-white color, were more than ten feet tall and wide and at least fifteen feet long. Each bulbous body was supported by six rather small legs that looked far too weak to support its bulk. He remembered that the microscopic insects these creatures resembled fed on minute flakes of human skin, and that realization sent a shudder through his body.

What Cris didn't know was that several hours earlier, about a dozen of these huge, insectlike creatures had appeared out of nowhere and stormed through the quiet little resort town of Delavan in one purposeful mass of horror, trampling and mangling every man, woman and child in sight. Now, by early evening, they had split into smaller groups and moved out of town, into the area around the lake where hundreds of families, including Cris Holman's, had homes.

One of the "bugs" turned away from the group, toward Cris, and in the diffused moonlight he got a good look at the thing. He almost gagged at the sight of the creature's head, especially its disgusting mouth parts. He noticed that the creature had some kind of tentaclelike appendages that seemed to wave about aimlessly, as though looking for something to latch onto. Fortunately for Cris, the creature didn't seem to notice him, and it turned back toward the rest of its group.

The sound of breaking glass shattered the night air. One of the things had pushed in a front window and was trying to force its bulky body through the opening.

"Mommy!"

The voice was faint but shrill. Cris was sure it belonged to Sara, and he knew he had to get to her somehow.

The monster that had broken the window withdrew its head, tentacles wiggling deliberately in the air, and turned to continue moving along the side of the house. The others were all doing much the same thing, moving slowly around and apparently looking for ways to get inside.

When all but one of the creatures was out of sight around the other side of the house, and he thought the remaining monster was far enough away from the front door, Cris made a dash in that direction.

He turned the knob, intending to duck inside, but the door was locked. "Sara, it's Cris! Let me in, quick!" He looked over his shoulder and saw one of the creatures coming toward him.

"Oh, God! Someone please let me in!" he screamed, frantically pounding his fists against the heavy wooden door. The door swung open, and

Cris dashed inside and slammed it hard behind him.

Marc Holman embraced his son. "Thank God you're all right!" he cried.

"What's happening here? Where are Mom and Sara? What *are* those things?" Cris, terrified and breathing heavily, fired off his questions in rapid succession.

"Your mother and Sara are in the rec room. Come on!" Marc Holman grabbed his son's arm and pulled him in that direction.

As they approached the doorway, Lois Holman and Sara came dashing out toward them. "Oh, Cris!" Lois cried happily while Sara simply ran to her brother.

Cris scooped Sara up in his arms. "Make the bugs go away, Cris. Please!" Sara sobbed as she held him tighly around the neck.

"Don't worry, Sara. Everything will be okay," he said, with much more confidence than he felt. He set Sara down and smoothed her hair. Then, turning to his father he asked again, quietly, "What *are* those things?"

Marc Holman shook his head. "I don't know. They just . . . appeared a while ago. We thought if we stayed quiet, they'd go away."

More glass shattered, this time somewhere in the rear of the house.

"What are we going to do?" Cris asked anxiously. Another window broke, this one only about ten feet from where they were standing. A cluster of obscenely writhing tentacles thrust itself through the opening. Sara screamed wildly and Marc Holman had to shout above the din.

"C'mon, let's get out of here! We should be safe in the basement." Marc Holman quickly ushered his family out of the room and followed them toward the basement stairs.

As they walked past the broken window closest to the basement stairway, Cris could see a pair of huge tentacles waving around outside. "Hurry!" he said, giving Lois and Sara a gentle push toward the stairs. He had one foot on the third step when Marc Holman's scream stopped him dead in his tracks.

Cris turned back toward the sound, but before he could react, a pair of tentacles had wrapped themselves around his father's body and dragged him halfway through the window.

"Dad!" he shouted as he leaped back up to the top of the stairway. But by that time Marc Holman was all but out of sight. His screaming stopped abruptly. Just as Cris started to lean through the window opening, he was distracted by his mother's screaming.

"No!" Lois Holman shrieked, taking the stairs two at a time.

"They got Daddy! They got Daddy!" Sara cried, following close behind.

When Lois reached the top of the stairs she

grabbed a ski pole off a rack on the wall and ran across the room toward a window where she could see one of the creatures trying to get in.

"Mom, don't! Come back!" Cris yelled after her, but she wasn't listening. He grabbed Sara as she reached the top of the stairs and held the terrified little girl tight. Then he watched in silent horror as his mother began jabbing at the thing with the pointed end of the pole.

"Get out!" Lois screamed. She managed to hit it two or three times, but the wounds had no apparent effect. In her frenzy she failed to notice that the creature's tentacles had circled around and were about to close on her body.

"Mom! Look out!" Cris cried another warning — too late.

One of the tentacles wrapped around the woman's neck, another about her waist. Cris instinctively shielded his sister's eyes and looked on, transfixed, as the thing tightened its grip and began to pull his mother out the window. Cris felt the bile rise in his throat and kept Sara's eyes covered as the gruesome being dragged Lois Holman's slender body out into the cold.

Fighting back the urge to go after his mother — which would have meant leaving Sara at the mercy of the monsters — Cris picked up his sister and ran with her down the stairs into the basement. The child kicked and fought to get free of her brother's grasp, but he held her tightly.

"Let me go! I want Mommy!" Sara screamed as she struggled to break free.

"Stop it!" Cris said sternly. Suddenly, as though all the strength had gone out of her, Sara's shrieks turned to quiet sobs. She collapsed against her brother's body. Her tear-filled eyes still showed her shock and horror, but now there was a look of resignation behind them.

Cris carried her to a windowless corner of the basement and set her down on the floor. He walked over to the other side of the room and began to pull a large, wooden table over to her, hoping that the scraping sound would not attract any attention. He pushed the table against the wall and used a small bookcase and a couple of chairs to form a shelter around the child.

Cris crouched down in front of the small opening he had left in one side of the shelter and spoke to Sara in a soothing tone. "I'm just going to go over and look out the window — but don't worry, those things are too big to get in any of the windows down here. You stay quiet and I'll be right back. Okay, sweetie?"

Cris felt his heart ache as he looked into Sara's large, green eyes. She had always trusted him to protect her. But the look on her face at this moment was one of absolute despair. He reached out and put one hand on her shoulder. There was little time to waste, and he had to make her listen. "Sara, I have to look around a little bit," he repeated. "I want you to stay here and wait. Do you understand?"

The child, who appeared to be in a state of shock, just stared at her brother — almost as though she did not recognize him. "Sara!" Cris said again, more sharply this time. "Please, Sara, listen to me! I want to be sure you'll be all right." Sara did not respond.

Hoping that what he said had registered somehow, he gave the little girl's shoulder a gentle squeeze. He turned and headed for a basement window on the other side of the room. He looked straight ahead out the window without opening it, then turned his head slowly from side to side. One of the creatures passed through his field of vision, moving from left to right as though it was patrolling along the side of the house, looking for other signs of life.

These things aren't going to go away by themselves, Cris told himself, fighting to stay rational. He looked across the room at the makeshift hiding place and thought about the way his father and mother had been grabbed. He decided that, in order to keep the same thing from happening to Sara, he would have to find some way to distract the creatures and lead them away from the house. That would mean leaving her alone, but he could think of no other way.

He crossed the basement back to where the child was hidden, crouched down, and spoke to her again. "Sara, I have to go outside. I have to leave you alone for a little while."

That statement seemed to bring Sara out of her stupor. She turned her head toward him and whimpered, "No!"

"I have to," Cris said, relieved that Sara now seemed capable of understanding his instructions. "I want you to stay here until I come back for you."

"Don't let them get me." The tone of the command lacked emotion, but the plaintive look in the child's eyes made Cris even more determined to save her.

"I won't, Sara. You can count on it." He crawled beneath the table, gently kissed the child, and then extracted himself from her hiding place. He walked back over to the window, saw that the coast was clear for the moment, slid one of the glass panels to the side, and cautiously pulled himself up through the opening. He squatted behind a row of partially trampled bushes and looked from side to side. Now that he was outside the house, he had a better view of the immediate area. And what he saw shocked him more than anything he'd already witnessed.

Off to his left, at the end of the driveway, he saw that his mother was still in the grasp of the creature that had dragged her through the window. She was kicking her legs feebly and softly whimpering. Lois, who moments before had expressed outrage at the violent death of her husband, now seemed to be facing a similar fate. And the ugly creature was being none too quick about it.

As the monster held the woman immobile, it began to change part of its form. Two of its tentacles were becoming shorter and thicker, right before Cris's astonished eyes. It took all of the self-control he had to keep from running out toward the creature and trying to free his mother. But he knew there was no way he could fight it, and he had to worry about Sara now. So he stayed quietly hidden behind the bushes, trembling with fear and rage, and watched and listened.

It took some time for the creature to finish its transformation. As he watched, Cris thought about his parents and how much he cared for them. He couldn't remember ever having told his father how much he loved him. And now it was too late; he hoped, but didn't expect, to see Marc Holman alive again.

After being abandoned by his mother when he was just a toddler, Cris had only his dad to depend on for several years. Then, when Cris was ten, Marc Holman had married Lois Anderson — and no one could have been more delighted than Cris. No natural mother could have treated her son better than Lois had treated Cris. The only thing missing after his father's marriage had been the brother he had always wanted.

Neither Cris nor his parents would ever forget how he had cried when Sara was born. He found the disappointment bitterly hard to accept — at first. And he vowed he would never love the pink little bundle Marc and Lois Holman brought home from the hospital. It took a little more than ten minutes for him to break that vow. Once Cris held his little sister, he fell head over heels in love — and his feelings for the little redheaded beauty only grew stronger with time.

They had been a real family — and an unusually happy one. Marriage did not cut into Cris's and his father's time together. But it did give Cris the benefit of the maternal side of parenting that he had never known.

Lois Holman loved both of her children intensely, and there was never a day that passed when she didn't tell them. She and Cris developed their own special bond, and Cris found it quite easy to share his day-to-day experiences with her — as well as some of his innermost feelings. It was a good life.

Now it was over. So quickly.

Cris's thoughts snapped back to the present, as he began to perceive exactly what was happening to the creature's shape. The tips of the stubby tentacles had split and were elongating into what looked like claws or pincers. He could tell by the moonlight reflecting off the creature's body that the claws were developing a rigid, glossy outer shell, in contrast to the flatter, leathery sheen of the rest of its body. As the claws continued to harden, the creature began to open and close them, as if exercising its newly formed appendages.

Cris couldn't stand it any more. "Mom!" he screamed as he burst from the bushes and ran toward the creature, hoping that he could get the thing to release his mother and come after him instead.

"Cris! Run!" Lois Holman cried weakly. She kicked more furiously now, finding a reserve of strength as the monster turned its attention, momentarily, toward her son. The other three giant-sized insects began moving methodically toward Cris, seemingly attracted to anything that moved. But the one trapping Lois Holman remained where it was.

"Run, Cris!" the woman repeated, more urgently this time. "Please, run!"

Cris thought again about Sara, and remembered that he had promised to keep her safe. He tried to convince himself that since the monster had not yet seriously harmed his mother, maybe it did not intend to kill her. He decided to go through with the plan he had formed to protect Sara and hoped that he would return later to find his mother alive.

Just before he turned to run away from the house, hoping to draw the creatures as far away from Sara as possible, Cris took one last hurried look at the only mother he had ever known. And then he cried, as loudly as he could, "I love you!"

It was the last thing Lois Holman ever heard. A second later, as Cris looked on in helpless horror, one of the monster's newly formed claws reached out and removed her head from her body.

It smiled. This was going to be easier than It had thought. Soon It would have a new home to add to Its list of many.

4

Nora Whitaker turned the key in the lock and pushed the door inward, withdrawing the key and stepping across the threshold of her apartment.

This one was not much different from any of the other dwellings she had inhabited in the last several years. And no matter how nicely decorated or how well furnished they were, they all had one major flaw in common — not one had ever come furnished with another walking, talking, breathing human being waiting to greet her on the other side of the door. They were all empty of everything except the material trappings. And after all these years, Nora was no more accustomed to the quiet of an empty apartment than she had been when she started this assignment.

She opened the dishwasher and took a clean

glass from the rack. "What's it going to be tonight, Nora?" She asked the question aloud, partly from habit, partly to fill the empty, quiet nothingness that had been her constant home companion for most of her adult life. She walked over to the small, L-shaped bar and studied the bottles lining the shelf behind it.

She would choose a bottle — it really didn't much matter which one at this point — and then fill her glass and drink the caustic sedative until she was just numb enough not to care that there was no one to talk to; no family to surround herself with; no one to fill the empty half of the bed she rarely used.

She poured some brandy into the eight-ounce drinking glass she had removed from the dishwasher and then slumped down on the couch, pulling her feet up onto the plush cushions.

Nora sloshed the liquid around in the glass, another habit, and then took a long, satisfying sip. She had no work to do tonight, so she was starting her "unwinding" a little earlier than usual, but otherwise the routine was much the same. People drink to forget — was that the old expression? Or was it drink to regret? Either of the terms was probably appropriate.

She should have been drinking to celebrate on this particular evening. There was certainly cause for that — at least in some respects. Another Cyborg Commando had been born today.

"Cheers!" she said, raising her glass, a tinge of sarcasm evident in her tone.

After undergoing surgery for nearly forty hours, John Edwards had a new name, a new body, and this success had breathed new hope into the Cyborg Commando program. Of the few dozen implant operations that had been performed successfully thus far, not one volunteer had come out of surgery with the immediately healthy mental attitude that this young man had exhibited. In fact, the minute his vocal circuits were connected he began facetiously trying to proposition the computer terminal standing closest to him.

Nora smiled. What a waste of a good man, she thought, and then mentally chided herself for that attitude. When had she stopped thinking her work was all-important? When had she stopped taking any pride in the part she had played, and continued to perform, in the development of the ultimate defense weapon? When had she given up thinking about winning a Nobel Prize and started mechanically perfoming her duties? When had she started drinking on a nightly basis?

"I definitely drink to regret," she concluded aloud, again raising her glass as if to make a toast and then finishing the rest of its contents in one angry, determined gulp.

Nora Whitaker was a woman who, at first glance, seemed to have more going for her than most women her age. But then, Nora did not allow most people to get a close enough look to be able to see what her life was really like, what it was that haunted her on almost a daily basis. And she intended to keep it that way.

Only a handful of people through the years had found out that Nora had once been married. To whom, she never divulged. "You wouldn't know him anyway," was her standard response. The marriage had broken up after a short time, but no one who knew that knew why.

Nora got up and walked across the room to pour another drink. She was in a melancholic mood, and the alcohol wasn't helping to offset it. This night was going to be another long, lonely one, and she would need all the liquid help she could get.

She poured more brandy into the glass and went back to the couch, this time carrying the half-empty bottle of liquor with her. "No need to get up any more than necessary," she sighed as she allowed her body to sink back down into the comfortable cushions. She lay back against one of the side pillows, took another drink, and then set the glass down on the marble coaster on the end table closest to her. She closed her eyes and tried to think of something — anything but what day this was. It didn't work. She sighed again and reached for her glass.

He was on her mind tonight, and it was hard for her to think about him without her liquid reinforcement close at hand. She couldn't help thinking about him tonight — she always thought about him this time of year. His bright little face with the big, blue eyes and silly little grin was permanently etched in her memory. She smiled, remembering the way he used to grab his toes and squeal with sheer joy. He was seventeen years old today, almost a man, and she ached to see him again — even if only at a distance.

Nora wondered what he looked like now. Did he have his father's red hair? He didn't have *any* when she had left him. . . .

"Oh, hell! Why am I doing this to myself?" Nora asked loudly, purposely interrupting her own thoughts. She picked up the bottle and was about to pour more of the brandy into her glass when her videocommunicator beeped. She got up quickly and walked across the room to turn the system on. A videotext indicator flashed across the 19-inch monitor and Nora watched with detachment as the words began to appear on the screen.

UPDATE ON C-12. AUGUST 19, 2032, 7:20 P.M.

THE PATIENT IS IN GOOD CONDITION AND SEEMS TO BE EXPERIENCING LITTLE DISCOMFORT OR EMOTIONAL TRAUMA. C-12 WISHES TO SEE YOU, DOCTOR — THIS EVENING IF POSSIBLE. HE SAYS THE TWO OF YOU HAVE SOME "UNFINISHED BUSINESS." THAT IS ALL.

WAITING FOR A REPLY. . .

Nora laughed. She quickly tapped out the message on her keyboard:

TELL C-12 I'M GLAD HE'S DOING SO WELL AND THAT I'LL SEE HIM TOMORROW. THAT IS ALL.

She waited a few minutes for confirmation that her message had been received, and for the end sign signifying that no further communication would be coming at this time. But there was another message — this one direct from C-12.

TELL LT. WHITAKER THAT I COULD USE SOME MOTHERING TONIGHT — THAT REALLY *IS* ALL!

The former John Edwards had no idea what that short message did to Nora's emotional state. She flashed the end sign across the screen without sending a reply, walked across the room and picked up the bottle of brandy. She finished what was left without bothering to pour the contents into her glass. And then she cried. She shed pools of hot, bitter tears for herself — and for the son she had left behind.

5

January 13, 2035

Cris ran. And as he ran, he cried.

He cried for his parents, who had died so horribly in the clutches of some nightmarish monsters that couldn't possibly be real . . . but were.

He cried for Sara, who at that moment might have been suffering the same fate — or who, at best, would spend the rest of her life painfully reliving this day many times over.

He cried for himself, and longed for his life to return to the way it had been but a few, tranquil hours earlier.

Despite the fact that the weather was not conducive to crying, the tears rolled freely down Cris Holman's face as he struggled to stay ahead of the hideous things that were pursuing him through the snow.

Cris tried to convince himself that he was just dreaming or suffering some kind of delusion. This was not happening! It was impossible! Somehow he had fallen asleep, or maybe he was still unconscious from hitting his head on the car window. He just had to stay alive long enough to wake up.

No. . . . This was no dream. As much as he wished it had been, what was happening was far more real than even the most brilliantly vivid of nightmares. Cris knew he would not be saved by an alarm clock or by the sound of Sara's voice telling him to "Wake up, you lazy bum!"

He ran. More accurately, he plowed through the foot-high snow as fast as he could manage, barely able to see where he was going. The monster bugs followed close behind. They were slower in the snow than he was, his years of athletic training giving him an edge over the clumsy creatures.

He tried to push his family out of his mind for the moment. He had to find a way to get the monsters as far away from the house as possible and then lose them so he could double back and rescue Sara. The only plan that entered his mind was based on the size of the creatures.

He had grown up in this area, and he knew exactly where to lead the huge, monstrous enemies so that they would have a hard time following. He turned in that direction, toward an area of dense woodland, where the pine trees were spaced a few feet apart. Finding the place came as much by instinct as by sight, for the weather was still causing some visibility problems.

Cris approached the area of the woods where a large human had to navigate carefully in and out of the maze of trees. He stopped at the edge of the densely forested area, then turned to make sure the creatures were still on his trail.

"Over here, you slimy bastards! Come and get me!" Cris reached down and picked up a handful of snow, forming it into a tight ball, and then threw it in the monsters' direction. He made several more, pelting the creatures until they were close enough to watch him duck into the woods. Then he waited.

They seemed to amble along, their bloated bodies almost too much for their disproportionately small legs to support. Once they got to the edge of the stand of trees, they shuffled around briefly on their tiny legs and tried to push their way through several narrow openings.

As he stood only a few dozen feet away from the spot where the nearest of the unearthly beings was located, Cris tried to communicate with the creatures.

"What are you? Why are you here?" he yelled.

The only response he got was the soft scraping sound of their bodies pushing against the trees that kept them from getting to where Cris stood.

"Why do you want to hurt me? Why don't you just tell me what you want?" Cris pleaded with the monsters, who either could not or would not respond to his questions. "What are you?" He screamed the question, his grief and frustration getting the best of him now. He leaned against the trunk of one of the trees and sobbed unashamedly as the creatures continued to try to reach him.

After a few seconds Cris regained his composure and stood very still, staring at the creatures as they kept trying to force their way through openings too small for their bloated bodies.

How many of these creatures were there? he wondered. Were there hundreds, thousands, millions like them roaming the earth? Or was this an isolated attack? A freak occurrence of some other lifeform lost and somehow deposited here on Earth? How could he get them to go away? He leaned back against one of the tall pines. He was safe, for the moment, and exhaustion had begun to set in.

The things had stopped moving. They were very still now, almost to the point of inactivity.

Cris picked up a short, heavy stick and threw it at the motionless form nearest him. The thing still did not move. He threw another and then another and still got no reaction. All movement had ceased outside his protective woodland retreat. But why?

Cris wondered whether the creatures were dead or if someone — or something — had simply turned them off. He eased a little closer, only a few paces separating him now from one of the ugly monsters. There was movement, just a flicker at first, but it was there. The creatures appeared to be . . . deflating? No, not exactly. . . .

Squinting at the body of the one closest to him, Cris could see that the outer surface was becoming puckered, drawing in on itself. At the same time, the thing appeared to be oozing a clear liquid that ran in rivulets along the crevices in its irregular surface and dribbled onto the ground.

The creature didn't act like it was injured, so Cris assumed that it was throwing off the liquid on purpose. Its body was just as tall as before and just as long, but was getting thinner from side to side. Then he realized what was going on — the thing seemed to be dehydrating, reducing its bulk. Soon it would be slender enough to pass through the opening that it was wedged against.

Cris glanced quickly to the side and off in the distance and could see that the other creatures were going through the same kind of change. Instead of waving about, their tentacles were lying harmlessly on the snow-covered ground. The way it looked, the creatures would remain inert until their transformation was completed. How long would that take? Cris wondered, feeling a sense of relief mingled with extreme urgency. A minute, an hour, a day? Was there time to make his way back to the house and rescue Sara before these things came back to life, maybe even more deadly and terrifying than before?

Whether there was time or not, he certainly

couldn't stay here and wait until they had made themselves thin enough to reach him. He had to take a chance.

Cris took the obvious precaution of exiting the woods a few hundred feet from the point where he entered, avoiding having to walk among the shape-changing bodies. Once he was clear of the dense growth, he picked up his pace and quickly made his way back home — to the one thing left there that was worth risking his life for.

When he got within sight of the house he approached it cautiously, in case there were any creatures lurking about other than the four he had lured into the forest. He didn't see or hear anything, so his confidence grew with each passing step. He came up to the back of the house, ducked his head, and entered through the same window where his father had been grabbed only a short time earlier. He ran down into the basement, careful not to make any unnecessary noise, and hurried over to where he had left his sister.

He crouched down next to the makeshift structure and there, huddled beneath the table where he had left her, was the little girl, looking as passive and emotionless as she had just before he left her earlier.

"Sara!" Cris cried, reaching in, grabbing the child, and pulling her toward him. He was too relieved at finding her alive to notice that Sara did not grab him back. Her small, limp body slouched in his arms. And her eyes showed no sign of recognition or relief.

Cris held her at arm's length. "Now listen closely, Sara. Whatever those things are, at least they're a little ways away from here right now — but they'll probably be back. We have to get out of here, okay?"

There was no answer. Her eyes showed no sign that she understood what her brother had just said to her. Cris took a close look at his sister. All of the relief he had felt at finding her alive gave way to a feeling of dread. She seemed utterly unwilling or unable to communicate.

"Sara! It's me, Cris! Sara, talk to me! What's wrong with you? What happened while I was gone?"

There seemed to be no life left behind her vacant stare. "Oh, Sara," Cris Holman sobbed as he held his catatonic sister gently in his arms. "I'll get those bastards for this. I promise you, baby, whatever it takes, I'll get them for this — and for two other people who'll never know it."

It smiled. Its arrogance far exceeded his.

6

October 20, 2033

"Someday all of this gadgetry may come in handy — but for now, what good is it?" John Edwards mildly complained as he carefully lowered his cybernetic body onto the couch in Nora's living room. After more than a year of living as a reconstructed technological wonder with no apparent purpose, John was beyond frustration. "I keep telling them, either put me to some good use or let me go back to being a normal human," John said.

Nora stared at the mixture of man and machine. She was frustrated by her inability to help her friend. She had been one of those responsible for developing the hundreds of cyborgs in the world. But now no one seemed to know exactly what to do with them, and scientists had yet to discover a way to reverse the brain-transplant process.

Operational cyborgs were useful after a fashion, but only in ways that the cyborgs themselves considered mundane or demeaning. For instance, C-12 had, in the last few months, seen intermittent service as an excavator on a government construction site. ("A bulldozer with lasers, but still a bulldozer," as John had put it.)

He had been used as the point man on a military bomb squad, until some general decided that C-12's arms and legs were worth more than a human soldier's life.

He suffered through a stint of crowd-control duty, until some other general realized that a cyborg used in that capacity wasn't doing any good for the image of the program.

Most humiliating of all, he spent a mercifully short time on the lecture circuit as a prop — forced to stand by soundlessly and, on cue, demonstrate the powers and abilities of his new form while some scientist expounded on his — no, his body's — virtues.

Nora knew what John had been through, and she couldn't help feeling guilty. "I'm sorry, John," she said as she poured herself a drink — a habit that C-12 had witnessed all too many times but had never questioned.

The two were in Nora's apartment, where they spent a lot of their evenings lately. They had become very close friends, the cyborg and the lady, despite their obvious differences.

"I don't mind having been one of the pioneers who proved that it is possible to build a better man, albeit part machine. But hey, now what do I do? Sit and twiddle my thumbs until—"

"No!" Nora said sharply. "At least not in my apartment. I don't need any laser-driven holes in my walls." She grinned, hoping that her teasing would get his mind off his feelings of frustration.

C-12 issued a weak, metallic chuckle. "Funny lady. But then, you can afford to be — you're walking around with a real, live body."

Nora smiled sympathetically. "Hold on a while longer, John. I know this program seems like a mistake to you, but I'm convinced we'll find a way to reverse the brain transplant soon. Just try to be patient."

C-12 was quiet for a while. All that could be heard was the sound of ice clinking in Nora's glass. Finally the cyborg spoke. "Do you know, dear lady, that you are the only person on the face of this screwed-up planet who ever calls me by my human name?"

"I'll work until the day I die, John, looking for a way to get you back to normal," Nora said with as much conviction as she could muster.

John Edwards believed she meant every word. But at the moment he had no hope of ever being reunited with his human self.

7

January 13-14, 2035

Even in his half-panicked state, it took Cris only a minute or so to figure out what he needed to do next.

Cris pulled Sara out from beneath the table, lifted her unresisting body, and trudged up the basement stairs. Still holding the child, he rifled through the closet near the front door for the flashlight he knew was always there. He turned it on and was quickly able to locate Sara's winter coat. With clumsiness partially caused by his desire to get everything done in a hurry and partially by his inexperience at doing such a thing, he pulled the sleeves over her thin arms, then fastened the coat around her torso and set her down gently on a chair in the large family room, as far from any windows as possible.

"I have some things to do," he told her softly. "You be good and wait right here, and I'll come and get you in just a few minutes." Sara just kept staring straight ahead, only her shallow breathing and the occasional blinking of her eyes giving evidence that she was alive and conscious. Even though he was worried by the way she sat, all but lifeless, Cris consoled himself with the thought that what he had to do would have been much more difficult if Sara had been crying, screaming, and trying to move around.

He went into the kitchen and tried the phone. As he suspected, the line was dead.

Help wasn't going to come from outside, at least not easily or quickly. He had to get away from the house with Sara, and he could only do that quickly and safely if he could get his father's four-wheel-drive truck running. First order of business: find the keys.

Cris pulled open a cupboard door and groped around toward the back of the top shelf until his fingers closed around what he was looking for — a thin ring holding a pair of keys for the truck, one of many spare sets of keys that were secreted around the house.

A gentle, sad smile passed over his face as he remembered how Lois, who consistently locked herself out of house and vehicle, had insisted they have at least two extra sets of keys made for every door in the house and for her car, her husband's truck, and even the car Cris drove. "You never know when you may lose them, and then you'll be happy to have the extras," she had said once, and then had made a face at her husband and stepson when they exchanged knowing looks.

"I know exactly what you two are thinking, and you're wrong," Lois had continued in a self-satisfied tone. "Why would I insist on keeping an extra set of keys in the house if, as you say, I'm afraid of being locked outside of it? That doesn't even make sense!"

"No, it doesn't," Marc Holman had said, a smirk spreading across his pleasant features. "But it's very sensible to hide keys under doormats, on closet shelves, in the refrigerator, and taped to the bottom of the mailbox!" he said, triumphantly producing a handful of miscellaneous keys from behind his back.

Cris smiled again, remembering how Lois had blushed and then had commanded her husband to "Put every last one of those right back where you found it!"

"Oh, don't worry, babe," Marc Holman had said, putting his arms around his embarrassed wife and winking at Cris behind her back. "I didn't dig up any of the keys you probably have planted all around the front yard."

Cris remembered how he and his father had roared at his poor stepmother's expense. It hurt to have such a pleasant memory in the midst of the pain he was suffering, because the recollection only seemed to make the pain even worse. . . .

It took all of two seconds for that reminiscence to flash through Cris's mind — two seconds that he scolded himself for wasting as he trotted to the front door. He opened it slowly, peered out to make sure nothing stood between him and the truck, and then bolted a few feet through the snow to where the vehicle was parked.

Judging from the pristine blanket of snow that covered it, Cris assumed the truck was undamaged. His mother's car, parked in front of the truck, was in the same condition; apparently neither vehicle had been moved all day. As he idly wondered why the creatures had not bothered at least investigating the two vehicles, he yanked open the driver's door, hoisted himself up onto the seat, and inserted the key in the starter lock.

He expected no less, but was relieved all the same when the engine immediately hummed with life. That brought to mind one of Marc Holman's most memorable quirks — his constant desire, which Cris had often referred to as an obsession, for keeping all of his family's vehicles in perfect working order. The driver batteries were never allowed to drop below half maximum charge; likewise, the tank of distilled alcohol that was used by the secondary propulsion system was topped off from the storage tank buried under the driveway just after one of the vehicles was brought back.

"Damn!" Cris cursed at himself under his breath as he abruptly shut off the engine. The electric-powered vehicle ran very quietly, but any noise was significant out here in the woods, where the normal condition in the dead of winter was absolute silence. He had only meant to keep the truck running for a second or two, to avoid attracting the attention of anything that might be within hearing distance — but now he had wasted another few seconds reminiscing, and might have put himself and Sara in jeopardy by doing so.

He grabbed the snowscraper from under the driver's seat and got out of the truck. He gently closed the door and then stretched across the front of the truck and cleared the snow off most of the windshield. After doing the same thing on all of the other windows, stopping every few seconds to listen for sounds of movement from the distant trees, he went back in the house and took a minute to check on Sara. She had not moved.

Next stop: the kitchen, again. He filled a heavy plastic bag with whatever food he could grab quickly from the pantry shelves and the refrigerator, not bothering to worry about what had nutritional value and what didn't. He left the bag of food by the front door and bounded up the stairs to the second floor, where his and Sara's rooms were located.

He went first to his sister's bedroom and threw open her closet door. He grabbed several items of clothing from hangers and threw them across her bed. He pulled out a drawer from her bureau and turned it upside down on the bed, emptying it of small garments and the trinkets that little girls habitually accumulated. He gathered up the corners of the bedspread and tied them together, forming a large bundle.

Then he did the same in his room, and in less than fifteen minutes altogether he was thumping back down the stairs, dragging two loads of what would have to pass for necessities. There was no time to gather valuables or memorabilia, no time for decisions of any except the most basic sort. Now that he had taken care of food and clothing, it was high time to find a new shelter.

The choice of where to go was really no choice at all. Cris wanted to — he had to — get back to Whitewater, back to reality and to the security of Maura's loving arms, both for his sake and his sister's. Sara had always enjoyed being with Maura when they got together on family outings or holidays, and Cris hoped that Maura's affinity for the little girl would help him bring her out of her near-catatonic state.

"Be right back, Sara," Cris said as he scurried past his sister on the way to the front door. He made two trips to the truck to load the food and clothing, stuffing it all in the storage area behind the seat, and then went back in for Sara. She was still sitting just as he had left her, arms limp at her sides and half-open eyes staring out and slightly down. Cris was unnerved every time he looked at her closely, and had to force himself to keep that feeling out of his voice. He knelt down beside her and touched her arm.

"Sara, we're going to take a little trip, to see Maura. You remember Maura, don't you?" Cris thought he saw her eyes flicker in acknowledgment, but then the moment passed and he couldn't be sure whether it had actually happened, or whether the near-darkness had played a trick on his eyes. "You can go to sleep while we ride, and you'll feel better when we get there," he said, more for his own peace of mind than for the sake of consoling her. She seemed, for the moment at least, to be beyond consolation, beyond reassurance. All she wanted to do (and perhaps "wanted" wasn't the right word) was to sit quietly and stare vacantly, as though she was trying to block out the memory of what had happened, and the only way to do that was to block out everything else at the same time.

With an inaudible sigh, Cris got to his feet, then bent over and scooped Sara into his arms. A glimmer of hope came into his heart as he felt his sister's arms ever so lightly and ever so gently embrace his neck. She didn't actually hold on to him, but there was no doubt in Cris's mind that she had moved her arms. Whether it was a reflex or a conscious movement didn't matter — it was a reaction, and any sort of reaction was better than none at all.

"We're gonna be okay, Sara. We're gonna be okay." With his mouth an inch away from her right ear, Cris kept up a patter of soothing words as he carried her out of the house, opened the passenger door of the truck with his free hand, and laid her on the seat. She pulled her legs up into the fetal position — another reflex? — and then lay still.

"Are you cold, Sara?" Without waiting for an answer, Cris added, "I'll go get a blanket." The area around the house was still deathly quiet, so Cris decided it would be safe to leave her in the vehicle while he made one last dash inside. He ran back inside the house, bolted up the stairs, pulled the one remaining blanket off Sara's bed and — feeling a bit ashamed of himself for not thinking of it earlier — wrapped one of her favorite stuffed animals inside it.

"I don't know how to take care of a child," he mumbled to himself as he trotted back down the stairs. "Maura will know what to do, though," he muttered, and that thought made him feel a little better.

Cris turned the knob, then shoved the door open with his shoulder. He left the house, pushing the door shut behind him, and trudged out to the truck. He climbed into his seat, wrapped Sara's arms around the fluffy white rabbit he had taken from her room, covered her with the blanket, and then started the engine. This time he didn't care about the noise, because he intended to be far away by the time anything could trace the sound back to its source.

He turned on the headlights and squinted reflexively for a second as his eyes were exposed to the first bright light they had seen since this nightmare began. He carefully backed the truck out of the driveway, grateful for the vehicle's eighteen-inch ground clearance that made it look ungainly but allowed it to move easily through the deep snow.

The wind had died down and the snowfall had tapered off quite a bit by now, so that as Cris looked out the side window of the truck, the scene before his eyes was almost pastoral: a cozy-looking house on the edge of a forest, being gently buffeted by a light snowfall as it was framed by evergreens with their branches bent under the weight of the snow they had caught. It would have been a beautiful view, except for the broken windows through which no lights were shining, the trampled bushes and hedges, and the gouges in the snow cover showing where the monsters had traveled as they mounted their murderous assault.

Cris tried not to see those things as he looked at his home for what might be the last time. He wanted to remember it as it should have been, not as it was. Bracing himself, he deliberately turned his gaze to the front and inched the truck ahead

until, out of the corner of his eye, he could tell that
the house was now out of sight.

* * *

It had taken them a full hour, but the creatures
trying to squeeze into the wooded area where Cris
had hidden earlier had adapted to their new situation. They literally dried out, expelling water to
make themselves smaller, and at the same time
re-forming into narrower shapes that would enable
them to pass between the trees and continue their
singleminded pursuit.

* * *

Cris had no trouble keeping the truck on the
road; there was a world of difference between driving this vehicle and his own car, which was much
more suited to a race course than to a snow-
clogged country road. From where he sat, his eyes
were only about as far above ground level as they
would have been if he was walking, but being this
high up while he was sitting in an enclosed space
gave him a strong sense of security along with
moderately good visibility.

He glanced over at the small child huddled next
to him on the seat, her head poking up out of the
blanket. He reached out and put his hand against
Sara's upper back. Her breathing seemed to be

deeper and a bit more regular. Then she stirred slightly and thrust out her right leg, an unconscious change of position that convinced Cris she was asleep.

That didn't take long, he thought, estimating that they had pulled away from the house only about ten minutes ago. "All she needed was to get out of that place," he said to himself.

He stayed alert for signs of other creatures or anything else unfamiliar, occasionally scanning the countryside, but kept his attention mainly on the road in front of him. He was very cautious about his speed, trying not to exceed twenty miles per hour as the big, thick-treaded tires churned their way through the snow. Visibility was still not all that great, and he didn't want to risk overdriving his headlights the way he had done when he had the accident in his car.

He reached over and pushed the power button on the radio, thinking a little music might help soothe his shattered nerves. Since he couldn't hear a signal on any of the pre-set stations, Cris assumed they were simply off the air — but that didn't make sense; according to his watch, it was only about ten o'clock. Fighting to stay calm, but feeling a quiver run through his hand despite himself, he started gingerly sliding the tuning lever from left to right. Finally he picked up a signal that seemed to be coming from far away and was frequently interrupted by static:

". . . state of emergency. Take shelter — underground, if possible — immediately! The entire planet is apparently under attack. . . . not a joke or a publicity stunt. This is the real thing!

"To repeat, the world is under attack. According to the Associated Press, a vast number of bombs were dropped in every part of the world beginning at approximately 4:52 a.m. Eastern Standard Time. These bombs were not nuclear warheads, but some kind of . . . ."

Cris shuddered, and could hardly believe what he was hearing. The entire planet! He thought back to the horror he had witnessed at his house, and tried to imagine that kind of wanton devastation and murder magnified millions of times — which made him shudder all over again.

". . . various shapes and sizes, all able to move under their own power, all of them intent on killing any human beings they can find. The most devastated area is the continent of Asia, where it seems that most of the 6.8 billion men, women, and children have been killed or injured . . . ."

Cris stopped the truck when the signal broke up this time. He was shocked and scared, and needed to steady himself before he could keep driving. Also, he didn't want to drive out of range of the signal before he had heard everything the announcer had to say.

". . . for the last several hours. As far as we know, this is the only superstation still broadcasting within a five-hundred-mile radius of Chicago, and our power might not last much longer. In this part of the country, communications facilities seem to have been very hard hit. The city of Chicago was apparently a primary target; in addition, some small and medium-sized cities have been overrun by swarms of creatures that scientists have not been able to identify.

"To repeat: Anyone within the sound of my voice should prepare for an extended state of emergency. Take shelter immediately. The entire planet is apparently . . . ."

The signal faded out again, and Cris turned the power off. It sounded like the man was starting his message over, and Cris had heard all he cared to hear anyway.

"Well," he said with determination, "at least I know where we stand." He was shattered by the news he had just found out, but the new knowledge didn't change his plans. He pressed gently on the accelerator, and the truck once more began to crunch its way smoothly and slowly through the snow. A few minutes later his curiosity got the better of him, and Cris turned on the radio again. This time he couldn't pick up anything but dead air and weak static.

An object on the side of the road suddenly became visible in the field of illumination thrown out by the truck's headlights. Cris drew in his breath sharply and almost hit the brakes. Then he saw the glint of light off metal and realized he was looking at his car — sitting right where he had abandoned it several hours earlier. He came up alongside it, nudging the truck to the left side of the road so that he could get around the front of the damaged vehicle, and gave what he could see of the car a quick visual examination.

Everything looked the same as he had remembered it, except that the car was now almost completely covered by a thin layer of new snow. He was relieved to find that it hadn't been disturbed, either by men or by anything else.

Then he noticed the tracks.

There were two long gouges in the snow, one on either side of the car, running parallel to the way the vehicle was facing. These indentations, with the snow piled up along the edges of each one, looked very much like the tracks that ringed his house — the gouges left behind when the monsters waddled along on their too-small legs, dragging their distended bellies through several inches of snow.

Suddenly he put it all together. He had collided with one of the creatures as it plodded across the road, either not able or not bothering to get out of the way of his car. The impact had not hurt the thing, at least not very much, because it had kept moving, and that was why he couldn't see what he had collided with when he had recovered from being stunned. And, apparently some time after he left the car and started walking, another of the things had come along, following the same route.

The interior of the truck was well heated, but that didn't prevent an uncontrollable shiver from racing up Cris's spine as he thought about what might have happened to him if he had been seriously injured in the crash, or if he had not abandoned the car. . . . In all likelihood, neither he nor Sara would be alive right now.

Cris purposefully took a series of deep breaths, gripping and releasing the steering wheel as he did so in an effort to get some of the tension to flow out of his body. When he felt more relaxed, he started to drive again. "Nonstop to Maura's from here on out," he said to himself.

Because he was driving the truck, he felt confident that he could navigate the route he normally took, despite the fact that he had trouble earlier that day trying to keep his car on the series of curving, small country roads. He was moving along at a steady twenty miles per hour, and had traveled close to ten miles on the small road he chose to take, when he discovered a large tree that had fallen — or perhaps been pushed — across the road.

Thanks to his slow speed, he had no trouble stopping in time to avoid hitting the tree. But he almost put the truck in the ditch along the side of the road when he tried to turn it around and get headed back the way he had come. Then he took the next turn to the left, figuring he'd head north until he found another road that went west toward the city.

After a few miles, he ran into another roadblock — this time, a massive snowdrift that filled a dip in the road and certainly would have brought the truck to a stop if he had tried to plow through it. Fortunately, Cris knew the road, and when he saw a level patch of ground where there should have been a depression, he recognized it for what it was. He stopped, laboriously turned the truck around again, and, not wanting to take any more chances, backtracked all the way to the highway that, as he now told himself critically, he should have used in the first place.

The journey continued without further incident until he was about five miles outside the city. Cris saw some shadows stretching across the road, and a couple of seconds later he felt the truck go over a short series of bumps.

"I didn't see anything in the road. So what'd I hit?" he muttered, bringing the truck to a stop and looking back over his shoulder. He could make out enough in the muted glow of the truck's yellow taillights to recognize more monster tracks.

These furrows seemed to be narrower and deeper than those he had seen before, indicating they probably had been made by a different kind of creature. This observation was enough to pique his curiosity and make him decide to investigate more closely. After a brief check of the still-sleeping Sara, Cris grabbed a lantern from behind his seat, climbed down out of the truck, and walked back to the tracks for a closer look.

When he played the light downward and over the furrows in the snow, he saw that his original observation was accurate. There were at least a half-dozen separate tracks, some overlapping and partially obscuring others. Each track was three to four feet wide, compared to the five- and six-foot-wide gouges that the monsters who killed his parents had left behind.

Remembering the "various shapes and sizes" part of the radio announcer's description, Cris deduced that these tracks had been made by either a different kind of creature or a smaller version of the grotesque, tentacled mites he and Sara had escaped from.

As it turned out, he needn't have spent those few seconds speculating. Cris brought the lantern beam up until it was almost parallel to the tracks and pivoted so that the intense light followed the grooves in the snow out across the flat field beside the road. At the very fringe of the illumination, he saw them.

At such a distance, the sight was more like an "it" than a "them." He saw a wriggling mass of what looked like thick tentacles, the various tail ends all grouped together and all whipping or gently flailing back and forth across the ground — a movement that had something to do with their form of locomotion, Cris guessed.

He snapped the light off after his first brief glimpse, suddenly afraid that he had betrayed his location. Then he risked another brief shot of light, needing to know whether they were turning to pursue him. But they had continued to recede into the distance, moving slowly but relentlessly toward Whitewater by a much more direct route than the road he was forced to take. He could barely see them any more, and probably wouldn't have noticed them at all if he hadn't already known what he was looking for.

Cris ran back to the truck as a new feeling of dread washed over him. At least some of the creatures were heading for Whitewater . . . for Maura. Perhaps others had preceded them, he thought as a lump formed in his throat. For the first time, Cris consciously acknowledged the possibility that the people of that city, and especially the woman he loved, were experiencing the same sort of horror he had just been through.

"I should have gone faster," he said angrily, thumping his gloved fist against the truck's instrument panel. "I should have come this way in the first place, and I'd be with her by now." Sara stirred and whimpered softly as Cris spoke, so he kept the rest of his thoughts, his apprehensions and his regrets, to himself as he eased the truck's speed up to a risky thirty miles per hour and forced himself to concentrate on driving the rest of the way to White-water as quickly as he could.

It heard the reports on the few radio stations still able to send transmissions, and — despite Its arrogance — It was mildly surprised. It hadn't expected the triumph over these beings to be so absolute, and so quick in coming. . . .

8

Cris thought he had prepared himself for the worst, especially since he had already seen some of the monsters and what they could do. But he had no idea how bad it could get.

If Sara had not been with him, he would have acted differently. He probably would have put on the brakes and gaped in horror at the broken buildings and dismembered bodies in the residential section he passed through on the south end of town. Instead, he kept himself composed, forced himself to keep his eyes on the road.

Sara stirred in her sleep, turning her face toward the back of the seat. Cris pulled the blanket up around her ears and patted her back gently for a couple of minutes, until he was sure she was asleep again.

He drove on, carefully, trying to keep a lookout for any of the killer creatures while ignoring the carnage that flashed before his eyes. There were bodies hanging out of windows, bodies sprawled next to and on top of cars, bodies simply lying in the street where they had been flung or cut down trying to escape whatever had killed them. Cris tried to veer around them when he could, but sometimes that just wasn't possible, and he had to fight to keep his stomach under control.

As he got closer to the campus and closer to Maura's apartment building, Cris noticed that the severity of the destruction and the number of bodies were lessening. That gave him new hope. Now he could once again tell himself, with conviction, that the chance of her being alive and well was good. He remembered the last time they had seen each other, how wonderful it had been, and how very long ago. . . .

The roadblock brought him back to the present. As Cris slowed the truck down to a crawl, two men approached the car. They were carrying guns, and as they got nearer Cris could see that they had "MP" armbands around the upper sleeves of their civilian outergarments. Cris lowered his window.

"Hello, sir. Would you please step out of the truck?" the man closest to him asked.

"Why?" Cris asked hesitantly, a little afraid of getting out of the truck and leaving Sara.

"We're under martial law, sir. Please step out of

the truck — for your own good as well as that of others." The man raised his gun slightly, in an obvious move to show that he meant what he said.

The man couldn't have been much older than Cris, but a man who held a pistol that was within six inches and one finger-twitch of putting a very large hole in Cris's forehead was not a man to argue with.

Cris opened his door and stepped down onto the pavement. "My little sister is sleeping in there," he said, tilting his head in Sara's direction. "She's been through hell. Can you just leave her be?"

The man on the other side of the truck walked all around it, looking in the windows, his gun ready for action. He circled the truck and then joined Cris and the other man. "We'll try not to disturb the little girl, but we have to see what's in that package you have stashed behind the seat."

"That?" Cris said, relieved that they were apparently just searching the truck. "That's just our stuff, wrapped in blankets. There's nothing—"

"We have to check it out, sir," the younger of the two guards said politely but with firm resolve.

"But why? What are you looking for?" Cris asked, and then it suddenly dawned on him. "Do you guys really think I'd be driving around with one of those creatures in my truck?" he asked, his tone of voice indicating his astonishment.

"We don't know yet who — or what — is behind this invasion. Now, would you take the bundle out of the truck, slowly, and set it on the ground." It was more of a command than it was a request.

"Sure, anything you say. Just quit pointing that gun at me," Cris agreed, annoyance beginning to creep into his tone. He didn't blame these guys for being suspicious. They were just doing their jobs, he supposed, and because they didn't seem especially dangerous he wasn't really worried for his and Sara's safety any more. But he was desperate to get to Maura's apartment and make sure she was all right. And he didn't want Sara to wake up and be scared. He dragged the bundle of clothes out of the car and set it on the ground.

"Now open it and back away," the older guard ordered. The two were now holding their pistols with both hands, the guns aimed at the bulk on the ground.

Cris untied the ends of the blanket and opened it up, spreading it out on the ground. Then he stood back. "Are you satisfied — or do you intend to shoot my sister's clothes, just in case?" he asked with the sarcasm in his tone perhaps too obvious.

"Get the other one out," the younger guard said, ignoring Cris's anger.

"Aw come on!" Cris exploded. "I'm in a hurry here! The other one's the same as this except that the clothes inside it are mine. Now could we please get—"

"Get it out, sir, and stop stalling. The sooner we

have you checked out, the sooner you can be on your way." The younger guard again addressed him, while the older one now stared coldly and held his pistol aimed directly at Cris.

Cris was still angry, but not about to argue any more. No telling what might happen if he pushed these men too far. He took the other tied-up parcel out of the truck and repeated the unveiling process a second time. The two men poked at his belongings while Cris stood and glared at them.

"Everything seems to be in order," said the older man curtly, turning his attention away from the bundles in the snow.

"Sorry to delay you," said the younger guard to Cris apologetically. He helped Cris retie the blankets and put them back in the truck.

Cris climbed in and the same guard offered his hand in a show of friendship, while the other man kept an eye out for any signs of approaching vehicles. "The name's Tony — Tony Minelli," he said, a smile appearing on his face for the first time.

"Why the strongarm treatment?" Cris asked sourly.

"Hey, I'm sorry, man, but it couldn't be helped. We're just a couple of volunteers with a job to do. Those . . . things . . . went through here a few hours ago and wiped out half the town. No one knows where they came from or if they'll be back. But we're not taking any chances."

"I know, I know," Cris said, trying to dismiss him

with a wave of his hand. "I'm just in a hurry." He started the truck, put it in gear, and took off before the young guard had a chance to say more.

Tony walked over to his partner and shook his head sadly. "He's heading for one of the worst-hit sections of town. I sure hope that poor guy isn't looking for anyone who might have lived there."

His partner agreed, staring at the freshly made tracks in the snow. "If he is, then he's in for a pretty bad time, 'cause there's certainly nothing left living there now."

If It could have witnessed this incident, It would have been happy beyond description. Now men were pointing weapons at other men. . . .

9

January 13, 2035
8 a.m. CST

Nora's head began pounding the instant she awoke to the insistent beeping of her videocommunicator. A slender strand of sunlight had worked its way through a crack between the draperies and splayed across the width of the living room, indicating the beginning of a new day — a day Nora was not psychologically or physically ready to face.

The room spun lazily as she attempted to raise her head off the side cushion of the window seat where she had flopped shortly after midnight. She didn't remember passing out, but the throbbing in her head and the waves of nausea wreaking havoc with what was left of her stomach lining left little doubt in her mind that she had consumed more than her usual excessive amount of alcohol.

"Ohhh," Nora moaned, wishing she had the energy to swear at the beeping videocom. She clamped her hand over her mouth and forced herself up off the window seat, attempting to make a beeline for the bathroom. But she was no more than halfway across the room when the beeping of the videocom was joined by the buzzing of her door intercom. The combination of the two sounds made her head throb worse than it did already. Someone wanted to talk to her on the videocom, and someone else wanted to be let in, but both of them would have to wait.

She continued her singleminded trek toward the bathroom, hoping to reach the toilet before the contents of her churning stomach ended up decorating her living-room carpet. Several minutes later she emerged from the bathroom, weak and shaky but now able to make her way toward the screen above the still-buzzing intercom. She turned on the screen and was surprised to see the form of C-12.

She pushed the button releasing the lock on the door of the apartment building and muttered, "It's open. Just come on up," before switching off the screen. She released the lock on her own door and then walked across the room and turned on her videocom. A message instantly came into view on the screen:

NATIONAL ALERT
CODE ARMAGEDDON

13 JAN 2035

THE PLANET IS UNDER ATTACK BY UNKNOWN FORCES. PRIMARY CC BASE IN CHICAGO INOPERATIVE. AS PER COMMAND STRUCTURE, MANITOWOC MUST NOW ASSUME RESPONSIBILITY OF PRIMARY BASE OPERATIONS. YOUR ASSISTANCE IS NEEDED IMMEDIATELY. PLEASE RESPOND.

Nora didn't even hear the cyborg come up behind her. She quickly tapped a simple message on her keyboard.

COMPUTER MALFUNCTION SUSPECTED. PLEASE RETRANSMIT.

"It's not a malfunction, Nora." C-12's metallic voice made her jump.

"John, what's going on?" she asked as the videocom screen repeated its former message word for word.

"Get dressed. You're desperately needed at the base. I'll fill you in on the way," C-12 said and then added, "I think this new body of mine is going to end up coming in handy after all."

10

A small strand of very faint sunlight heralded the approaching end of the longest night Cris Holman had ever spent. The storm and wind had stopped. The ground sparkled with a covering of fresh snow, which made a crunching sound when Cris stepped on it.

Cris stood on the far east edge of the university campus, looking out upon one of the best views in town. He knew he should be inside the college's emergency shelter, where it was safe — if there was such a thing as a safe place to be these days. But Cris needed to be alone right now, so after making sure Sara would be well cared for in the shelter's nursery, he had headed for this spot.

A clump of trees in one area, a cornfield (now stalkless) in another, and a variety of symmetrical little hills and valleys — with a stream (now frozen and barely discernible beneath the snow cover) thrown in to top it all off — were neatly arranged, as though the pieces of scenery had been carefully sorted and organized.

The view was breathtaking, and it was one the chronically early-rising Maura had enjoyed on many occasions. She had even talked Cris into sharing it with her one morning after he had spent the night at her house.

"All right. I'll get up and go off with you, out in the freezing cold, at four a.m. tomorrow morning, and then maybe you'll quit bugging me, a dedicated night person, to get up before the crack of dawn to see any more sunrises, okay?" Cris had agreed, his tone implying phony disgust.

"Just wait! You'll love it so much you'll beg me to take you again," Maura had said.

"But—"

"But?" Maura moaned, interrupting him.

"But — in order for me to be awake at that hour, you'll have to keep me up all night," Cris winked, resting his chin in his hand and casting Maura a challenging look.

"No problem!" Maura had tossed back enthusiastically. They had been sitting at her dining-room table, attempting to study, but the attraction had been too great for either of them. Cris had been all too happy to slam his book closed and take Maura in his arms.

He smiled sadly now, remembering that night as well as the next morning. They had stayed awake all night, alternately making love, talking, and raiding the refrigerator. It had been perfect. And then they topped it all off by standing together in her favorite morning spot in the whole world.

"It's breathtaking," Cris had said, obviously surprised, and Maura had just smiled.

"I told you," she said, holding him close and staring out at the perfect landscape.

"Yes, but this goes beyond the definition of the word spectacular."

They had stood there for a full thirty minutes, holding each other, sometimes kissing, and once in a while commenting on the view before them.

"I'm so glad you brought me here," Cris said finally, as they were about to leave.

"Me too," Maura answered softly.

They were quiet for some time and then Cris spoke. "Maura, there's something I want to tell you." He took hold of her shoulders and turned her toward him, staring intently into her large, brown eyes.

"Not bad news, I hope," she said a little nervously.

"Far from it," he had answered, and then, without hesitating, he said, "Maura, I love you." It had been a lot easier than he had expected. The words came out as naturally as if he had said "good morning." And this was the first time he had spoken them to anyone other than the members of his family.

Cris shivered and wrapped his arms around his shoulders.

It was hard to believe his world had changed so dramatically in the course of such a short span of time. Only forty-eight hours ago he had been at home, a home that no longer existed, asleep and blissfully unaware that the world he had known was about to come to a terrifying end. And in its place was left a nightmare, filled with terror and chaos, and an unknown presence that seemed to be hell-bent on killing every inhabitant on the face of the planet.

He began walking back to the shelter on the university campus where he and Sara had gone after Cris had failed to find Maura.

Cris shook his head, trying to rid himself of the images that flashed through his mind. He doubted he would ever again be free of the disgusting pictures his memory had accumulated since the whole nightmare began.

Maura was dead. She had to be. There was virtually nothing left of her house. Whatever had come down her street had a lot of force behind it — or them. Parts of broken bodies lay strewn throughout her neighborhood and, although he had found no part that was recognizably Maura — after spending an hour performing the gruesome task of sorting through the carnage closest to her house

— he had found her ankle bracelet, still clasped and covered with blood. There was only one way that it could have come off her leg without being unfastened.

Cris closed his eyes tightly and tried to think about something else until a wave of nausea passed. He had become violently ill after finding the bracelet, and had been fighting a recurrence off and on through the rest of the night.

He took a deep breath and then sat down on the steps leading to the building that was currently housing about five hundred misplaced persons in its lower level.

He and Sara had come to the emergency center in the wee hours of the morning after learning about it from one of the many National Guardsmen roaming the city.

He was glad to have found a place where they could rest and be relatively safe. But the place was full of people all telling different versions of the same nightmare.

"My son went out to the garage to get a hammer out of his tool bin and he never came back," one distraught mother cried. "We heard him scream, but when we tried to go to him the whole back yard and alley were covered with these . . . things! My husband pulled me back in the house, and we hid in the basement until they went away."

"Did you find your son later?" asked a sympathetic listener sitting next to her.

"No," the woman answered, almost inaudibly.

One by one they told their tales of tragedy and horror. And since everything that had happened was so far removed from reality, it was still hard for Cris to believe that all of it was any more than a terrible dream.

Sara still didn't seem to be aware of anything around her, and Cris was beginning to wonder if she ever would again. When he had registered the two of them at the shelter, the woman who was handling the paperwork greeted her cheerily and asked her what her name was. Sara had stood next to Cris, her hand resting limply in his, and had not even batted an eye.

"Her name's Jenny," Cris had lied, hoping the child would correct him. But she didn't. He gave the correct information to the woman and guided Sara to their assigned cots.

Sara lay still for hours, her eyes open wide and staring. Cris wondered how much she really heard and understood of the conversation that was going on around her. He was hoping, for her sake, that she comprehended little or nothing.

She had fallen asleep again, finally, and he had sat up on his cot, his back leaning against the wall, listening to her breathe. Finally, when he knew the sun was about to come up, he decided to take a walk. Before leaving the shelter he asked one of the guards patrolling outside if it was safe to walk a short distance, and he was told that there had been no sign of the creatures all night. That was good news — or at least an absence of bad.

Cris got up and began walking up the steps. Sara would be awake soon and he didn't want her to be frightened or think he had left her. He was the only person she had now, and she was all there was left in the world for him to care about.

It watched, with a tinge of regret, as the dawn of a new morning slowly tracked across the continent known as North America. The first day of an assault was always the most . . . productive, and It was mildly sorry to see the day coming to an end.

11

January 16, 2035

"Look, all I'm saying is that we can't just sit here and wait for the food supply to dwindle to nothing, or for those . . . things . . . out there to figure out how to get at us. We have to do something, or it's a matter of time before we're all dead meat — and I mean that literally!"

The speaker was a short, middle-aged man with a thick mop of dark, curly hair. Under different circumstances he would have been considered pleasant-looking, his stature and natural ruddy complexion giving the impression that he was much younger than his forty-two years. But his features were far from pleasant as he tried to convince a group of about fifty men and women that they should take matters into their own hands.

"C'mon, Bettser, how are we supposed to fight

those creatures when we don't even know what they are?" one of the men in the group chided the determined self-appointed leader.

Now, three days after the city had been attacked, those hiding in the emergency shelter beneath the college's physical education facility were beginning to get restless. They were anxious for life to return to some semblance of normalcy. Some insisted on leaving the safe confines of the shelter but were warned by the guards at the exits that they could be risking their lives, and they might not be allowed to return whenever they desired if, in their words, "the shelter is already at capacity when you approach."

Space was not the problem; there were enough interconnected corridors and rooms below ground level to accommodate, at close quarters, thousands of people. Obviously, the word "capacity" was being used in relation to the available supplies of food, medicine, and other essentials. Someone had decided how many people could be fed and cared for without exhausting those supplies too rapidly. A continual count of the underground population was kept, and if the shelter was filled to capacity no one — man, woman, or child — would be admitted until someone else had left.

Word travels fast among a group of cooped-up people, and the policy about capacity was common knowledge within a couple of hours after it was put in effect. Still, a lot of people had left for one reason or another. Some of them wanted to look for friends or family members who might still be alive outside. Some wanted to get back to their houses or dormitory rooms and salvage any possessions they could carry. Some were claustrophobic, or just plain stir crazy — they *had* to get out.

Bob Bettser fell into none of those categories. He was, by nature, a person who found it difficult to sit back and let someone else solve his problems for him. And the way he saw it, he was one of millions of people who had a big problem and, as he put it, he had made up his mind to "do something besides hide." Now he was trying to convince others to join the cause.

Cris Holman sat quietly and listened as Bettser laid out his plans: They would leave the shelter, gather firearms and explosives from the homes of three of the men (two gun collectors and one so-called "survivalist"), collect some camping equipment, and set up headquarters in the wooded area around Whitewater Lake. From that base of operations, they would go out on seek-and-destroy missions, killing any monsters they came across.

"The man's right. We gotta do something." Tony Minelli leaned toward Cris and added his two cents' worth in a hoarse whisper. The young volunteer who had stopped Cris upon his arrival in Whitewater three days earlier seemed to be hanging on Bettser's every word, except when he wanted to add a few of his own.

Cris just shrugged, not quite sure what he thought of Bettser's idea. Tony tried again.

"The longer we stay here," he said, "the less chance we'll have of getting rid of those things. They aren't gonna go away by themselves, and from what I hear, the army is taking a pretty bad beating."

"What makes you think we can succeed where the army is failing?" Cris countered.

Tony was ready for that one. "The military is fighting them head-on, trying to wipe out groups of 'em all at once. They aren't worrying about loners or stragglers, 'cause it takes too much firepower, too much manpower, and too much organization to send out a lot of small squads to go after these things one at a time. Well, that's where we come in — our specialty will be picking off the isolated ones."

That comment had led to Cris's next question. "How are a dozen men with small arms and maybe a few explosives going to make a difference, even if they're good enough and lucky enough to kill one of these things every day?"

"I'm sure we won't be the *only* ones fighting guerrilla style," Tony said. "But we'll be doing our part — the least anybody can do. Or do you just wanna sit here and hope that everything will be all right? If everybody took that attitude, who'd be left to make that hope into a reality?"

Cris could have been offended by Tony's implied insult, or he could have reacted sarcastically to his hokey remark about turning hope into reality. But Tony had a non-caustic way of saying these things that, combined with the look of genuine earnestness on his face, made Cris feel a bit ashamed of himself.

Tony had approached Cris the day before, when Cris was leaving the center for a late-night walk. (His father's truck had been impounded by the military, as had all other civilian vehicles.)

"I wouldn't stray too far," Tony had said, turning his flashlight on and shining it in Cris's face, nearly scaring the young man out of his wits. He hadn't seen Tony standing off to the side of the building. He didn't hear him come up behind him, and he didn't appreciate the scare. But Tony didn't notice Cris's anger, just his face. "Hey! You're one of the people whose cars we searched the other day. Remember me? Tony Minelli?" The flashlight continued to shine in Cris's face as Tony extended a friendly hand. "I guess you were kind of mad that we stopped you, but geez, man, if you had seen what those monsters did to this city . . . ."

"I did," Cris said quietly.

"You were looking for someone. Did you have any luck?" Tony asked, although he was pretty sure he knew what the answer was going to be.

"No, my luck ran out a few days ago," Cris said, his tone laden with self-pity.

"Hey, you aren't alone, buddy, I'm sorry to say."

"Could you please point that flashlight somewhere else before you blind me?" Cris asked, feeling a little guilty for being so annoyed with someone who was just trying to be friendly. As soon as he made that remark, he wished he could take it back. But Tony didn't seem to be offended — or if he was, he didn't let it show.

"Oh, I'm sorry. It's just so damn dark, and I was raised with the benefit of electricity. It's hard for me to get used to not being able to see anything when the sun goes down." He turned off the flashlight and tucked it into one of the large pockets in his poncho.

"I don't mean to be rude, but I'm not feeling very talkative these days. I just want to be alone," Cris said. Then he turned and walked away.

"Hey, man, I understand. But don't go too far. It's not safe," Tony called after him. If Cris heard, he gave no indication.

The next time Cris saw Tony Minelli was the next day, when he had walked into the general meeting that had been called for everyone who was sequestered in the shelter.

"Hey! How was the walk? Glad to see you didn't run into any bug patrols," Tony said, his smile warm and sincere.

Cris extended his hand when the young man sat down next to him. "I suppose I've been rather unfriendly—"

"Rather!" Tony's response was followed by such

a warm smile that Cris realized it was meant to be taken lightly. For the first time in days, he smiled back.

Then the two had turned their attention to the front of the room where Bettser was asking for the floor. And for some time a hearty discussion about the pros and cons of forming a group of civilian fighters to deal with the threat of creatures in the immediate vicinity kept his attention riveted to the speaker of the moment. Until Tony challenged his sense of civic duty, or his intelligence — Cris was not really sure which.

He was about to respond to Tony's remark about his attitude when a newcomer suddenly spoke up, his tone one of practiced authority that commanded attention.

"I've been sitting here, patiently, listening to this bullshit about how the military isn't doing anything, and I can say — as someone who has firsthand information — that there are a lot of things you people don't know." The man was in his fifties, overweight, with pasty white skin — obviously not combat material, even though he wore an army uniform. His eyes darted back and forth, up and down, all around the room, as if he was assessing those present.

Bettser abruptly turned toward the khaki-clad man. "Then why don't you share your information, Sergeant . . . Hines?" he asked, squinting and leaning forward a bit to read the nameplate on the man's uniform. The older man strode to the front of the room and spoke in a clear, serious monotone.

"As I said, there are a lot of things you don't know, and a lot of things none of us can predict. The army is having a rough time of it right now, but we're still a lot better equipped to fight these . . . things . . . than you are." He paused, but no one seemed to have anything to say to that right away. So he continued, his voice more impassioned this time, his eyes flickering from one face to the other.

"Don't waste your energy, and risk throwing away your lives, trying to fight something that's bigger than all of you. If you really want to help, there's a better way."

"For instance?" Bettser shot back loudly, not in the least pleased with the turn the conversation was taking.

Sergeant Hines got to the point. "Up in Manitowoc there's an army research center that's been set up to deal with the production of a weapon so devastating that even these bug-things would be hard pressed to stand up against it. And all we need are the men to man the machines, so to speak."

"What kind of machine are we talking about here?" Bettser asked in a challenging tone.

Sergeant Hines was quiet for a moment and then, carefully choosing his words, said, "That may be a simple question, but the answer is definitely not."

"That's a cop-out!" A voice from the group rang out loud and angry.

"Cut the double talk!" shouted Tony, who was about to continue his tirade before Hines turned to him and glared at him so intensely that the young man decided to hold his tongue. Sergeant Hines took a deep breath, regained his composure, and then went on.

"I'm not trying to avoid answering," he said in a tired voice. "There really is no simple way to describe the process of transplanting a human brain into a computerized body. But if any of you have the time or the inclination to learn more about joining the Cyborg Commandos — a team so powerful that nothing on the face of this earth, or elsewhere, can withstand its force — then I'll be happy to fill you in." And with that Sergeant Hines left the room.

12

It took Cris about twenty-four hours to realize he had made a bad decision. By then, there wasn't much he could do about it.

His spirits had been high when he strode toward the exit from the shelter just after Bettser, the leader of the group, announced to anyone who cared to listen that "The Exterminators" had mustered up and were about to go forth.

They were bolstered even more when a couple dozen of those who were staying behind stepped up and wished him well or silently embraced him. So this is what it feels like to go off to war, he thought. No wonder soldiers are so willing . . .

The only hard part, in the beginning, was leaving Sara. Cris left her in the care of several of the shelter's occupants who had set up a nursery, of sorts, for any of the children who were there without their parents. The group, which consisted of three women and two men, seemed nice enough, and definitely responsible. But Cris was worried that, even in her unresponsive state, Sara would think he was abandoning her.

"Sara, I have to leave for a while. I'm going to help get rid of those bad monsters and then you and I are going to go away somewhere nice and peaceful. We're going to have a wonderful time together, just wait and see," Cris had told her before leaving the shelter. She still appeared to be in shock, so he had no real hope of her understanding what he said. "I'll be back," he said, and then left her with a woman whose own child and husband had been killed.

"We'll take good care of her," the kindly woman had assured Cris.

"Please keep telling her I'll be back soon, even if she doesn't seem to understand," Cris had asked, and then he added words of appreciation and gratitude for the woman and the others who would be caring for his sister.

"You don't have to thank me," the woman had told him. "Having someone to care for, something to care about, takes my mind off my own losses right now."

Cris knew exactly how she felt. In the midst of a world that would never be the same again, he had found two things to care about. He loved his sister and would do whatever he could to make sure she survived and recovered. But he cared almost as much about doing whatever he could to rid the world of the monsters that had ravaged it. There seemed to be nothing he could do for Sara right now — perhaps, he thought in his more depressed moments, she would never recover. So he had decided to follow, for now, the second path that beckoned to him.

In the beginning Cris had felt buoyant when he was trudging, with his cohorts, proudly through the debris-strewn streets of Whitewater — proudly, despite the fact that pitifully few people watched them as they walked, and fewer still cared what they were up to.

His spirits had flagged, but only a bit, when The Exterminators made the rounds of several homes, where the members of the group had expected to commandeer a regiment's worth of weapons and explosives. "Tom's got a regular arsenal in his basement," one man had said — but when the men got to Tom's house, the arsenal was gone. They salvaged a hunting rifle from the hall closet and a couple of boxes of ammunition from the kitchen cupboard. That scene was repeated, in essence, half a dozen times over, and each time the limited success was rationalized: "Somebody beat us to the stash, but that's okay; they're probably making good use of it."

Bettser was not a friendly man but he was charismatic, a good leader. He had the ability to keep people under his control and pointed in the direction he wanted them to go. When the list of "sure things" had been exhausted, and The Exterminators still didn't have enough weaponry to outfit everybody in the group, Bettser led his men on a house-to-house search.

For the next two hours, Cris and his companions performed enough misdemeanors to last the average petty criminal a lifetime. They broke into houses, unintentionally but uncaringly terrifying people who were huddled in basements, and ransacked closets, storerooms, and garages for anything they could use to add to their meager store of camping and survival supplies or enhance their killing capacity.

The result of all those illegal acts was not worth the effort, even considering that there was no danger of The Exterminators being apprehended or prosecuted. They finished their regulated rampage with a gain of one half-loaded handgun and six extra rounds of ammunition.

Because they still didn't have enough guns to go around, and because Cris was one of the last people to join the group, he was still weaponless as the group headed for the wilderness. "We'll get more firepower as time goes by," Bettser said to the men. "Nothing to worry about — every militia squad starts out undergunned and overmanned. Men are more important than guns."

Even after going through all of this, and still being unarmed when it was over, Cris kept himself convinced that he was exhilarated and that he had done the right thing. He had been placed in charge of one of the three first-aid kits the group had managed to scavenge, and Bettser had persuaded him that his role in the operation was just as essential as anyone else's. "If someone goes down," he said, "you'll be there to help him. If he doesn't get up, grab his weapon and take his place."

That bit of encouragement, if it could be called that, helped to keep Cris going through the late afternoon and early evening as the group made its way resolutely out of the city. His morale was also boosted by Tony Minelli, who stayed close to Cris every chance he got and kept up a stream of optimistic chatter that was uplifting even if it wasn't always logical.

"Now this is a lot more fun than being holed up underground, isn't it?" Tony said exuberantly. Although he was developing some affection for Tony, Cris didn't know him well enough yet to be sure whether he was consciously trying to cheer Cris up or whether this was just Tony's nature.

"We're not doing this to have fun," Cris countered, but not in an argumentative tone.

"True, my man, quite true. Myself, I'd rather be curled up with a good book — or preferably, a good woman. But we gotta do what we gotta do, and we may as well enjoy it."

"Easy for you to say. You've got a gun, but all I'm packing is a sleeping bag and a box of pills and bandages."

"Patience, patience," Tony said with cheerful condescension. "We'll find more guns — maybe tomorrow — and then you'll feel better. In the meantime, I'll hang close, won't let you out of my sight. If anything tries to gobble you up, old Tony will give it one right between the eyes. . . . Boy, I can hardly wait!"

"Patience, patience," Cris said, flashing a thin smile at Tony as he mimicked his words. Tony grinned back, and the two of them walked along in silence after that.

One of the men didn't make it through the first night in the woods. He woke up and staggered groggily out of his tent to relieve himself, forgetting to cry out so that the men on sentry duty would know he was moving around. He took five steps in the darkness, the snow crunching loudly beneath his feet, and then was suddenly jolted fully awake by a terrified voice screaming "Help!"

The cries were immediately punctuated by rifle shots as the guard emptied his gun in the direction of the noise he had heard. One of the bullets caught the man in the head, and he was dead before he hit the ground.

Nobody slept for the rest of the night, and not even Tony was in the mood to make any jokes. Once Bettser figured out what had happened, he congratulated the trigger-happy guard and used the incident as an object lesson.

"That's what happens if you move around in the dark without letting anyone else know what you're doing," Bettser said. "When you're on guard duty, you shoot first and ask questions later. If anyone's dumb enough to go for a nighttime stroll in the snow like that, he'll get what he deserves — and the rest of us will be better off without him."

That line of thinking didn't make sense to Cris. Hadn't Bettser just said, hours ago, that men were more important than anything else? For the first time, Cris began to have doubts about the man's ability to lead — and he didn't feel any better about it even after he was given the pistol that the dead man had been carrying.

As the next day dawned and grew into afternoon, Cris felt more and more trapped into something he didn't want to see through. They had no plan; all they were doing was traipsing around in the underbrush. They weren't equipped for an extended stay in the wilderness — two of the men didn't even have gloves, and the food they were packing wouldn't last more than another couple of days.

Bettser was either oblivious to the problems, or else he was choosing to disregard them. When someone suggested heading back into the city for another foraging expedition, he practically bit the man's head off. "We came out here to do a job, and we're going to do it!" he roared. "Nobody ever said it would be easy, but we sure as hell won't get anywhere with all of you trying to undermine my authority!"

That outburst even got to Tony. Cris noticed a worried expression on his face for the first time since they had left the emergency shelter. The light tone disappeared from his chattering, and he talked less frequently. When he spoke, it was usually only to mutter something like, "We oughta be spotting some of those things any time now." He was still determined, but didn't seem to be as hopeful.

At dusk on the second day, Tony's prediction came true. The point man in the formation trudged to the top of a steep hill and immediately threw himself to the ground. When the others came up even with him, what they saw brought back bitter, awful memories for Cris.

There were four of them, and from their appearance they could have been the same ones that destroyed his house and killed his parents: grotesque, ungainly things moving along the open terrain in the valley below the group of men. From this distance their short, spindly legs were all but invisible beneath their bulky bodies — but there was no mistaking the long, thick tentacles that extended from the fronts of their bodies, waving purposefully in much the same way that an elephant moves its trunk. Three of them were about the

same size — Cris estimated each to be about fifteen feet in length, ten feet high — and the fourth
one, bringing up the rear, was a bit smaller and
seemingly a bit slower than the others.

"Pretty much the way I thought they'd look,"
Tony whispered. Cris was surprised to find out
that, apparently, Tony had never seen one of the
things before. From other remarks he picked up
from the men around him, Cris gathered that most,
if not all, of them were also seeing the monsters for
the first time — and that realization, coupled with
his own personal knowledge of what these things
could do, drained away what little confidence he
had left.

Bettser motioned everyone back down the crest
of the hill and held an impromptu tactical session
— and Cris was upset, almost embarrassed, as he
realized that this was the first time they had ever
talked about exactly what to do when they came
across some of the monsters. At that moment, his
despair was practically as great as it had been
when he witnessed his parents' deaths.

"What we gotta do," Bettser said, "is split 'em
up, take 'em one at a time. Kill one, track the others, kill another one, and so on."

"Easier said than done," Cris mumbled.

"What was that, kid?" Bettser had overheard
him, and he didn't sound pleased.

Cris, discouraged but still intimidated enough
not to openly resist, thought fast. "I said, 'Start with

119

the small one,' sir," he responded, pausing briefly
before the last word and putting a slightly scornful
edge into it.

"I was just about to say that," Bettser snapped
back. "And I'll say anything else that needs to be
said. You just listen, and make sure that pistol's
got a full load."

It does, thought Cris, which is more than I can
say for you.

The plan was much simpler than Bettser's repetitious stream of orders made it seem. Cris and
Tony, the two fastest runners in the group (and
also the two youngest members), would come up
behind the monsters and try to attract the attention
of the smallest one without alerting the others. Assuming they did that successfully, they would then
encourage the thing to chase them, and they
would high-tail it to the nearest clump of trees,
where they could either hide or climb to safety.
Once the monster was sufficiently far away from
the other three, the rest of the men would come
storming down the slope, surround the monster,
and kill it.

Last but not least, Tony was ordered to relin-
quish his rifle to one of the men who was still unarmed. "He'll need it more than you will," said Bettser when Tony objected mildly. "Hold onto that pistol," Bettser said to Cris, "and use it to signal us if
you get lost."

"He makes it sound so easy," Cris said to Tony

as they made their way in roundabout fashion down into the valley.

"It does make sense, you have to admit that," Tony said in his usual optimistic tone. "I can even see the logic in giving up my rifle, since I can't run and shoot at the same time."

"Tony, nobody here knows what we're up against — nobody but me, and I don't know that much. Maybe these things can outrun us if they try to. Maybe they don't get hurt by bullets. Maybe we should realize that they're probably smarter than they look. . . ."

"And maybe they're not," Tony interjected. "All I know is, if we expect less than success, that's what we'll get."

"That sounds like a line from a sleep-tape on self-esteem," said Cris with a smile.

"How did you know?" shot back Tony, his face breaking into an even wider grin.

* * *

They did what they were supposed to, and it worked pretty well. By making conspicuous shuffling noises in the snow and slapping the fronts of their padded jackets with their hands, they made enough noise to be heard by the trailing monster but apparently not enough to be detected by the three others that were, by now, a good fifty feet ahead of the smallest and slowest one.

Cris felt a pang of terror pull at his heart when the monster began to turn toward them, and an even sharper pang when he thought he saw two of the others also swerve from their straight-ahead paths. But then they resumed their previous course, and Cris was almost relieved to see that, in fact, only the last one of the things was coming around to chase them.

"Okay, now we go!" Tony said under his breath, and both he and Cris started their hundred-yard sprint to a stand of trees nearby. Cris slogged through the shin-deep snow, not daring to take the time for a glance back over his shoulder and trying to concentrate on going as fast as he could without stumbling.

He foolishly held onto his pistol as he ran, and when the hand holding the weapon bumped against his leg, he dropped the gun into the snow. Tony, running a couple of steps behind, saw the gun fall and noticed Cris slow down for a second. "Forget it!" he said breathlessly, and Cris took his advice. When they got just inside the wooded area, Cris and Tony turned to see how close they had come to dying.

In fact, the gap between them and the monster was no smaller than when they had first started to run away from it — somewhere between thirty and forty feet — but, Cris thought with a shudder, it was no larger, either. The thing had been able to keep up with them even though they had been

moving as fast as they could go. Fortunately, they
didn't have far to travel; if they had been forced to
sprint two hundred yards instead of one hundred,
they might have been too fatigued at the end of the
run to keep from being caught.

The thing kept moving until it actually bumped
into an old, thick pine tree at the edge of the clear-
ing. Of course, by then Cris and Tony were several
yards farther back into the woods.

Cris scanned the woods around them, pointed
to a spot a few yards to one side where the trees
were smaller but more closely packed, and motioned for Tony to follow him in that direction.
"C'mon," he said.

"Those trees are too small!" Tony said, panting
and sounding panicky. "I'll stay here," he added,
crouching behind the girth of the thickest, lowest-
hanging evergreen he could find in the immediate
area.

"Trust me," Cris said emphatically. "I've done
this before. And hurry up — the damn thing's coming through the trees!"

So, Tony trusted him, and the two of them
watched from within their protective cover of spindly but sturdy pines as the creature shifted and
slid, haltingly finding its way through spaces between trees that were wide enough to allow it pas-
sage. The thing closed to where the leading edges
of its tentacles were about thirty feet away from
Cris and Tony, and suddenly the air was filled with

the sounds of noisy movement through the snow and war whoops from the throats of thirty-, forty-, and fifty-year-old men.

"Here comes the cavalry," said Cris.

"I hope they can all shoot half as well as they can yell," Tony grumbled, matching Cris's tone of sarcasm.

The creature that had been chasing Cris and Tony lifted the front part of its body and began to turn toward the men who were running up behind it. A couple of rifle shots rang out, but in the darkness Cris couldn't tell whether they had hit the monster or not. What he did realize, in the next instant, was that he and Tony were standing right in the line of fire. "Get down!" he yelled, giving Tony's shoulder a push as he flattened himself in the snow.

From his lower vantage point, the creature looked bigger than ever to Cris, even though the thing was several yards distant and moving away from where he and Tony were lying. With surprising speed and agility, it had turned around and begun to advance toward the gang of men who were descending upon it. The thing apparently had enough intelligence not to allow itself to be surrounded in the trees, where its mobility would be severely reduced.

The whooping and hollering subsided quickly, to be replaced by occasional curses and other brief utterances of fear and dismay as the men discovered that the creature was not going to let itself be taken from behind. Three more gunshots resounded, each from a different location along the men's fanned-out formation. From what Cris could see, the nearest of the men was still at least fifty yards away from the creature. Then he heard Bettser's voice.

"Get closer!" the leader bellowed. "Make every shot count!" Just as Bettser said this, Cris could see the men slacken their pace drastically.

"Don't stop! Keep going!" exhorted Bettser, now with a maniacal edge to his voice. "Come on, you cowards!"

The creature was moving on an angle away from Cris and Tony, threading its way between the trees at the edge of the wooded area. Cris could see most of the men clearly now, since the monster had moved out of his line of sight. All but three of them were standing in the open, seemingly transfixed by the unearthly sight before their eyes. Bettser and a couple of men on either side of him continued to move toward the thing, clumping through the shin-deep snow with their weapons pointed at the bulky monstrosity.

"Aim for the head!" Bettser shouted, apparently oblivious to the fact that only a couple of other men were still listening to his orders. Then the man raised his rifle and got off a shot that Cris was sure had hit the thing; it was now outside the trees, only about twenty yards away from Bettser. As if that was a signal for them, the men on either side of Bettser began to empty their weapons into the creature. Most, if not all, of the shots hit their target — and still the thing continued to move toward the men.

"I know I hit it!" said one of the men, panic-stricken. "Why doesn't it go down?"

"Shoot its eyes out!" roared Bettser. "Let it get closer!" The leader stood his ground and held his fire, his rifle poised on his shoulder. "One good shot is all it takes!"

"This one doesn't *have* any eyes!" said one of the men as he turned and began to run in the opposite direction.

"Come on, Bettser!" said the other one. "We gotta get out of here!"

Bettser didn't reply. Instead, he fired another shot at the creature, which was now less than ten yards from where he was standing. Like the other bullets before it, this one had no apparent effect. The thing seemed to twitch slightly from the impact of the shot, but kept moving methodically forward, its ten-foot-long tentacles waving obscenely before its path. At this point, the last of the stalwarts turned and fled, leaving Bettser standing alone in the snow. He yelled at Bettser once more to get away, but the leader didn't budge.

"Just one good shot!" Bettser repeated, as though he was trying to convince himself. Then he fired again, and this time the creature was so close that the flash from the rifle's muzzle illuminated the thing's tentacles briefly. When this shot also failed to bring the creature down, Bettser finally came to his senses — too late.

He dropped his rifle, pivoted, and tried to get away, but Bettser had taken only a couple of steps before the creature was upon him. One tentacle coiled around his thighs, causing him to fall into the snow. He screamed, and a couple of seconds later the sound was cut off as another tentacle wrapped itself around his chest and head. Then the monster moved its body forward while holding Bettser motionless on the ground. When the man was completely beneath the thing, it stopped, tucked its tiny legs under itself, and lowered its body down on Bettser in much the same way that a hen settles down on an egg. It was impossible for Cris to tell if Bettser had been crushed, suffocated, or consumed, but after a couple of minutes it was obvious that he was dead.

Some of the men had run away before Bettser's death, and now those who had stayed close enough to see what had happened to their leader were also giving up the fight. They began moving back up the slope they had descended with such vigor a short time earlier, traveling singly or in pairs and going as fast as the terrain and the snow cover would permit. They either had forgotten about, or didn't care about, the two young men still hiding in the grove of trees. Cris and Tony were in no immediate danger, but they were angry and scared nevertheless when they saw their comrades deserting them.

"What do they think they're doing?" said Tony, waving his arm in the direction of the fleeing men.

"They think they're saving their skins," said Cris with disgust. "So I guess it's up to us to do the same thing for ourselves." Even if he had the pistol now, he wouldn't bother firing it — and finding it wasn't worth risking a run across the open terrain in front of the creature.

The monster that had killed Bettser still hadn't moved from the spot where it stopped, and now even the motion of its tentacles had all but ceased. "Do you think it's asleep?" asked Tony, indicating the whitish-gray bulk that, when stationary, was practically invisible against the snowy wilderness.

"If I had to guess," said Cris grimly, "I'd say it's having a late-night snack — and we better get out of here before it starts moving again."

In order to follow the route the other men had taken, Cris and Tony would have had to cross the patch of open ground where the monster was stationed. So they took off in the opposite direction, staying in wooded areas as often as they could, and worked their way back toward the city.

Two hours after sunrise, the pair of very exhausted ex-militiamen were picked up at the Whitewater city limits by a National Guard truck and dropped off at the emergency shelter that they had proudly marched away from less than two days earlier.

It had received many reports of isolated, disorganized attacks on Its invasion force; the natives of this planet were apparently as fearless, in a foolhardy way, as they were stupid. But that knowledge only made It more pleased. Now that victory was all but assured, It would enjoy the diversion of an occasional, insignificant challenge. . . .

13

January 19, 2035

Entrance into the shelter was still being monitored to control the number of people who could be
inside. About two dozen men and women were in
line ahead of them, and Cris and Tony had to wait
for almost an hour and a half before they could get
back inside. Standing in the cold was, in a way,
even more taxing than the all-night hike they had
just been through, and both of them were nearly
out on their feet when they were finally admitted.
Without bothering to scout around for unoccupied
beds and unused blankets, they simply staggered
over to the base of the wall nearest the door they
entered, stretched out on the floor, and were
asleep in minutes.

The next thing Cris knew, someone was shaking his shoulder, and as he woke up he heard

himself shouting "No! No!" Cris opened his eyes and saw Tony crouched over him, one hand grasping his shoulder and the other one pulled back as though he intended to slap Cris's face.

"You were having a real bad dream," said Tony softly as his look of concern was replaced by a soft smile. "You were yelling loud enough to wake me up, and that ain't easy."

"Sorry," said Cris distractedly as memories of the dream came flooding into his conscious mind. From a distant vantage point between a couple of trees, Cris saw Bettser standing defiantly in the path of one of the monstrous creatures. The man was holding Sara in front of him, as though for protection. Sara was sighting down the barrel of a child-sized rifle, and Bettser was telling her, "All it takes is one good shot!" The monster came closer and closer . . . and then Cris forced the vision from his mind, not wanting to relive what had come next.

"How long have we been asleep?" he asked Tony, trying to get himself refocused on reality.

"I think about six hours," Tony answered after glancing at his watch. "Longer than a catnap, shorter than I would have liked. If you think you'll be okay now, I'm going to put my head down and pick up where I left off."

"You go ahead," said Cris, getting to his feet. "I have to get to the nursery and see Sara, make sure she's all right."

"You sure know how to make a guy feel guilty for just wanting to cop a snooze," Tony sighed. "We'll *both* go see Sara, and then we'll *both* get some more sleep, okay?"

"Okay," said Cris. "Thanks." Especially after what he had been through, Cris was glad to have a friend and companion, and he had a hunch that Tony felt the same way.

The two of them made their way through the shelter to the section where the unattended children were housed. Cris's jaw dropped in shock as he rounded a corner, peered through a doorway, and saw that the nursery was occupied not by children, but by small clusters of middle-aged and elderly adults.

"What's going on?" he said anxiously, accusingly, to no one in particular. "Where are the kids? Where's my sister?"

Nobody answered right away, and Cris was about to reach out, grab the nearest man by the collar, and start shaking him when an old man off to one side spoke up.

"Took 'em outta here yesterday," he said. "Food's runnin' short here, in case ya hadn't noticed. Army wanted t' make sure the kids didn't get shorted, so any ones that didn't have family to look after 'em got put on a truck. If ya had a sister in here, why didn't ya claim her when the call went out?"

Cris ignored the question. "Where did they go?"

he asked in a tone of desperation, his anger giving way to sadness and shame as he cursed himself for leaving Sara alone.

"Manitowoc," the man said. "Army's got some kinda big base up there, real well protected and full o' food an' beds, or so they say. Kids'll get taken care of, but in a few days the rest of us are gonna be on our own."

Cris muttered "Thanks for your help" in the general direction of the men who had spoken to him, and the two young men turned and left the room.

"What do we do now?" asked Tony.

"I'm going to Manitowoc," said Cris. "I have to find Sara. They never should have taken her without my permission."

"You can't really blame them," Tony said in a gentle tone, trying to get his friend to see the other side. "They didn't know you were coming back this soon. Hell, they didn't know if you'd be coming back at all."

"I'm starting to wish more than ever that I hadn't gone on the warpath with those . . . misfits." Cris's flash of anger had passed, and depression was setting in.

"Don't forget that I'm the misfit who talked you into doing that — which means that I'm as much to blame as you are." Tony looked up and fixed his gaze on Cris's eyes. "And the least I can do now is go with you and help you find her. The sooner we get moving, the sooner we'll be there."

Cris reached out and clasped Tony's shoulder in a gesture of appreciation that spoke louder than words.

*　　*　　*

For the next hour, Cris and Tony interrogated every man they could find who was wearing a military uniform. Most of the soldiers couldn't or wouldn't give out any information, but the two young men did manage to find out some important and useful facts . . . if they were true.

At breakfast the day before — the morning after Cris and Tony had left with Bettser's group — word came down from the officials in charge of rationing that the shelter's supplies of food and medicine were running low. Since there was no feasible way of replenishing the supplies, the decision had been made to evacuate the large number of children who were not housed with family members or relatives, as well as all of the ill or injured adults. They were to be taken to Manitowoc, where the army was operating out of a very large and very secure underground base that served as a research center for the Cyborg Commando Force.

Mention of that phrase brought back to Cris's mind what he had heard from Sergeant Hines a few days ago about the project to create super-soldiers by transplanting human brains into mechanical bodies. Tony recalled the same conversation, and he and Cris exchanged a few words about it as they sought out another soldier to question. They had both seen a cyborg once while attending the same lecture series at the college. The thing had just stood there, demonstrating its abilities on cue while some military spokesman talked about the program.

Although neither Tony nor Cris had known each other at the time, they both had the same first impression of the super-human — what good was it, anyway? It was obvious right away that Tony's attitude about the project had changed since the first time he had heard about it. And Cris, who had been mildly interested at first, now wished he had paid more attention.

"If this cyborg base is still operating, then either Manitowoc hasn't been visited by bug-creatures yet or the base is really well-equipped and secure," Tony theorized. "In any event, it sounds like a good place to take Sara and the rest of the kids. I think she's in good hands, Cris."

"That makes sense, but I'm still worried," said Cris. "This cyborg place sounds like just the sort of thing these monsters would enjoy wrecking. Maybe they don't know it's there yet, or maybe they're having a hard time getting into it — but when they do, everybody inside will be in big trouble."

"Don't say 'when,' my boy — say 'if'. We don't know that anyone up there is in any danger, and besides, these cyborg soldiers sound like they could do a lot better than Bettser when it comes to battling bugs."

"Bad assumption on your part," Cris retorted. "We know very little about cyborg soldiers, and practically nothing about the bug-monsters — except that rifle bullets don't stop them, even from point-blank range. I'll be glad to find out that a cyborg soldier can kill these creatures, but I won't believe it unless I see it happen."

"Okay," Tony conceded, "you can choose to be skeptical. As for me, I'd rather have some of those handy gadgets we saw on the cyborg guy who was here a few months ago. That built-in laser beam went through twelve inches of brick like it wasn't there. The artillery these Cyborg Commandos are dressed in has more of a chance of doing some serious damage to those — whatever they are — than anything else we have available."

From the next few soldiers they met, Cris and Tony learned that three civilian trucks carrying unattached children had left the shelter at about noon the previous day and were followed a few minutes later by a pair of semi-trailer trucks that had been outfitted as mobile hospitals and were fully stocked with invalids. The army didn't use its own vehicles because it wanted to avoid attracting attention from the bug-creatures, which seemed to have a special preference for attacking men and machines that were obviously military.

Also, each set of vehicles took a different route,

since the army had learned from tragic experience that the creatures seemed to be attracted to long caravans of vehicles but tended to ignore or disregard smaller groups. Although the creatures couldn't travel fast enough to overtake or keep up with moving vehicles, they seemed to have some way of passing along information to others of their kind.

One man told them a story, in grisly detail, of how the caravan he was in traveled for several miles through hostile territory. He could see groups of creatures off to either side of the road occasionally, but none of them seemed interested in moving to attack. Then, when the dozen trucks were traversing a long stretch of road with no turnoffs, the scout car leading the pack crested a small rise and was confronted by a double line of monsters arrayed across the roadway, waiting just a few hundred yards ahead. The convoy managed to stop and get turned around before the creatures could get close enough to do any damage, but just a minute later as the lead vehicle rounded a sharp curve, it came upon another cluster of the things blocking the road.

The two groups were obviously working in concert, and had planned their assault to take place on a section of road where the vehicles — and the men inside them — had no good chance to escape. The courageous but foolish driver of the lead truck tried to plow his vehicle through the ghastly barricade, and did manage to take a couple of the things with him before his truck skidded on the snow-packed pavement and then fell on its side, effectively blocking both lanes of the road.

Then the massacre began. The soldiers quickly found that their weapons were all but useless against the monsters, and they were doomed whether they stayed in the trucks or tried to get away on foot. Several dozen of the creatures had formed a loose ring around the trapped vehicles, and they tightened the noose with brutal efficiency and surprising speed. Pitifully few men survived, and they did so only by pretending to be dead or by fortunately being knocked unconscious, so that the creatures thought they were dead.

Cris shuddered. If he had known ahead of time just how formidable and intelligent these creatures were, he never would have gone strutting off with a ragtag bunch of men whose expectations were larger than the space between their ears — and Sara would be with him now, instead of somewhere a couple hundred miles away surrounded by people who didn't know her and probably didn't care about her.

"We try to warn people whenever we get the chance, but without adequate means of communication, it's all word of mouth, and there are only so many of us to go around. Anyone attempting to travel right now is taking his life in his hands. If you don't have to be anywhere, my advice to you is to get inside somewhere and stay there until we get this thing under control."

"Thanks for the advice, but I'm afraid we'll have to take our chances. I have to get to Manitowoc," Cris said with determination.

The last soldier they spoke to was sitting at a small table near the loading docks from where the trucks had departed the previous day. He had his head down, and seemed to be preoccupied with a small stack of papers he was shuffling through. When Cris and Tony got close enough, they recognized him as Sergeant Hines.

"Wait," whispered Tony when they were still out of earshot. "If this guy remembers me, he won't be too happy to see me."

"Just let me do the talking," Cris murmured as they approached the table. Then, as the man looked up, he added, "Hello, sir."

"Can I help you, gentlemen?" The man's voice was cordial, but he sounded tired.

"I hope so," Cris answered. "We need a way to get to Manitowoc so I can find my sister."

Sergeant Hines' face brightened visibly at the mention of the city. "I can get you a free ride, leaving tomorrow morning. All you have to do is sign this paper authorizing us to put you through preliminary testing," he said, thrusting a blank form in Cris's direction.

"Testing?"

"For the Cyborg Commando Force. Let me tell

you . . . . Wait a minute — haven't I seen you two before?" the sergeant said, peering closely at Tony's face.

"We heard you talk about the program a few days ago," said Cris in a friendly tone, anxious to keep the conversation civil.

"Hmmm. And at least one of you wasn't especially impressed."

"Not at the time, sir," Tony admitted. "But I've kinda changed my mind since then."

The sergeant allowed himself a wry smile, but didn't say what he was thinking. "And what about you?" he asked Cris.

"I'm not convinced," he replied honestly, "but I guess I'd like to know more about it." If catering to this man was the only way to get from here to Manitowoc, Cris thought, then he would do his diplomatic best to achieve that goal.

"That's all we ask," said Hines. "Fill out these forms, sign them, and return them to me by 0600 tomorrow. The truck leaves an hour later." The sergeant seemed to want to end the conversation at that point, but Cris wasn't done.

"My sister is in Manitowoc," he said. "She was taken out of here yesterday. I need to find her."

Sergeant Hines sighed heavily and dropped his eyes. "Don't know what to tell you except that it's risky traveling out there. Some of our trucks have made it through — and some of them haven't."

Nothing could offset the awful feeling that was

growing in the pit of Cris's stomach. "Why can't we leave right away?"

"We've been hit by one hell of a snowstorm all day," Hines explained. "The snow's letting up now, but for our own safety we can't travel at night. The best we can do is to leave at sunrise."

Cris wasn't satisfied with that, but he was too emotionally and physically drained to get into a fruitless argument. "Come on, Cris," said Tony, taking his friend by the arm. "Let's get some rest." He picked up a couple of the forms from the sergeant's table, nodded a good-bye to the man, and led Cris away.

The mechanical task of putting personal information down on the form took Cris's mind off his worries, but only briefly. He spent the night staring at the ceiling over his cot, waiting for the morning to come and dreading what might happen when it did.

14

Cris Holman sat languidly on the floor of the truck. His face was impassive, his eyes open but cold, giving no hint of the emotional turmoil he was going through.

If he had wanted to try, Cris could not have described how he felt at this moment, as the truck rumbled through the streets on the outskirts of Manitowoc. His feelings changed almost instantaneously as his emotions seesawed and fluctuated, like a crazily oscillating pendulum that was swinging back and forth and around in a circle at the same time.

He was relieved when the driver of the truck announced that they had arrived in Manitowoc, but he didn't join in the cheer that went up from most of the other passengers. He was glad that he had

survived the trip, but guilty for feeling that way . . .
because poor Sara had not been so lucky.

More than anything, Cris was crushed and grief-
stricken. His pessimistic anticipation had turned to
brutal shock when, about fifty miles northwest of
Whitewater, the truck he was in had come upon a
scene of carnage unlike anything he had ever
imagined. Three trucks, half-covered with snow
from yesterday's storm, were resting at odd angles
beside and across the road. Cris knew without
being told that these were the vehicles that had
carried the children away from Whitewater. So it
came as no surprise when he overheard the soldier in the back of the truck tell another passenger,
"Those are the trucks that were evacuating those
kids from the Whitewater shelter." It was obvious
even from a distance that no one inside them could
still be alive.

Two of the vehicles were lying on their sides,
and on one of those the metal top had been torn
and peeled back to expose the space where the
young, defenseless passengers had been contained. Cris's truck slowed to a crawl as the driver
threaded his way through the wreckage and the
bodies, most of them small ones, that were strewn
for several yards in every direction around the disabled vehicles. For a few horrible seconds he
stared out the back window of the truck he was in,
looking directly at the pile of small, frozen corpses
that had partially spilled out of the overturned

truck. He fought back the urge to vomit, forced himself to keep from shaking with rage and terror, and kept his eyes glued to the scene, searching in vain for some sign of life, some sign of his little sister.

Cris's truck stopped briefly a few hundred feet beyond the wreckage, and he saw soldiers from the vehicle following his truck disembark and make a cursory examination. From the way they went about it and the short amount of time they spent at the task, it was obvious they didn't expect to find any survivors. If any children had been left alive after the attack, they certainly could not have lived through two winter nights and one daytime snowstorm.

As the truck began to move again and the awful view behind him shrank into the distance, Cris's vision blurred as his eyes filled with tears. Aside from a smattering of muttered curses and expressions of disgust and horror, the twenty passengers in Cris's truck were silent. Cris began to sob, and his shoulders shook. Then Tony, who had been beside him at the rear window, led Cris back to a seat along the side of the truck. Cris's head dropped between his knees, and for the next few minutes the tears came freely — not that Cris could have stopped them if he had wanted to. As though from a long distance away, he heard Tony softly explain to the people around them that "His sister is back there."

When he had cried all the tears he had to cry and the initial shock had subsided, Cris felt himself consumed by rage. "I want to kill them all," he said to Tony, his fists clenched so tightly that his fingernails were cutting into his palms.

"I'm with you, buddy," his friend said sympathetically.

*   *   *

The conversation in the truck got louder and more animated as the vehicle rolled eastward, deeper into the city and closer to Lake Michigan. Everyone was glad that the trip was almost over. Cris came out of his lethargy and forced himself to start thinking about where he was and what he was going to do next.

From what he could see out the back window of the truck, the city of Manitowoc seemed pretty deserted, but in a placid way. He noticed abandoned vehicles, lots of broken windows, and some houses and buildings that had been damaged. But he didn't see any dead bodies; he supposed that either the city hadn't been hit too hard, or the army had been very efficient about recovering the victims.

When the truck reached the fringe of the downtown business district, the driver wheeled it around a sharp corner and then slammed on the brakes. The passengers let out an uproar as many of them were thrown to the floor by the sudden stop, and a couple of people started pounding on the wall that separated the passenger compartment from the front seat, demanding to know what was going on.

That question was answered, in part, a moment later when the guard that had been riding up front with the driver unlatched the back door and flung it open. "Everybody out!" he yelled, brandishing a grenade launcher. "Get away from the truck and spread out!"

Nobody needed to be told twice. The truck emptied out in a matter of seconds, and when Cris and Tony got alongside the vehicle and looked out to the front they saw what had brought the truck to a halt.

Two of the bug-creatures were about half a block away. One of them was moving slowly across the four-lane road, almost waddling as its distended underbelly bumped and dragged along the pavement. The other one, smaller in size but identical in proportions, was following behind and slightly to one side, farther from the truck. Neither one seemed aware that the truck and its former occupants were only a few hundred feet away.

"The guard says to move to the side of the road and take cover. If they keep going, we get back in the truck in a few minutes," said the man next to Cris and Tony in a stage whisper. "If they start to head this way, we start running like hell. Pass it on."

Tony conveyed the instructions to the young man on the other side of him. Then he and Cris trotted to the curb and crouched down behind the front of a car with four flat tires and a caved-in roof. Cris noticed that the driver's door was ajar, pushed out of its frame by the force that had crushed the roof, and when he glanced down he noticed a small pool of frozen blood right beneath the opening. He made a point of not looking in the window.

The only sounds Cris could hear were the almost inaudible hum of the truck's generator and the loud, disgusting, scraping and squishing noises the monsters made as they pulled themselves across the road. These two looked more bloated than any of the others Cris had seen, and with each passing second it became more and more apparent that they weren't going to bother coming after the truck or its passengers.

"Do you think they don't know we're here?" whispered Tony.

"Could be," Cris answered. "More likely, I'd guess that they've just . . . that they're full, and that makes them less aggressive."

As though it was confirming that assumption, the creature in the lead stopped momentarily, shifted the front of its body slightly toward the truck, and wriggled its tentacles. Cris tensed and froze, ready to whirl and head in the opposite direction if the monster came even one step closer. But that didn't happen. The thing lifted its tentacles and raised the front of its body, in a gesture that looked almost haughty, and then resumed its lurching movement in the same direction it had been going.

The thing was almost off the roadway, and its smaller companion was just beginning to move onto the broad sidewalk adjacent to the street, when Cris heard a loud *whump* — followed almost immediately by an explosion and a gout of flame that shot up out of the far side of the larger creature's body.

His first impression was that the soldier with the grenade launcher had decided to take a shot, and he immediately cursed the man mentally for drawing the creature's attention in his direction. Then he realized that the shot had hit the monster in a place the soldier couldn't have targeted on, and for the next second or two he was more bewildered than anything else.

"Look at that!" Tony's voice was a shriek, but one of amazement instead of terror. Cris's gaze went out along the length of Tony's pointed finger. There, in full view, standing atop the flat roof of a two-story building a few doors down the street, was a . . .

"What . . . the . . . hell?" Cris breathed. The figure, dressed in what appeared to be armor, looked about seven or seven and a half feet tall. He was standing with his legs apart and his arms held out straight, pointed down toward the monsters. Before Cris could think about the impossibility of what he was seeing, another *whump* reverberated through the air and another explosion sounded — this time from the body of the second monster!

"It's a cyborg!" shouted someone hiding a few yards away from Cris and Tony.

"A cyborg *commando*," corrected Cris in a low voice, awe and envy written all over his face.

Both creatures had been hurt but could still move. In a reaction of either reflex or panic, the larger one had immediately begun to turn away from the direction of the cyborg's attack. The thing pivoted around on its spindly legs, apparently trying to double back along the path it had just taken across the road. As it turned its wounded side toward Cris, he could see a gaping hole in the creature's flank. The flesh inside was soft, oozing, and glistening, quite unlike the thing's leathery, shell-like outer skin. One of its legs had been blown away, and as Cris watched another leg crumpled beneath the thing, apparently not strong enough to support the weight of the body any longer.

The cyborg got off two more grenades, seconds apart, and both of the monsters were literally blown in two by the followup shots. They were immobile now, their rear sections lying inert except for the convulsive thrashing of their remaining legs. The tentacles extending from the fronts of their bodies were flailing wildly, beating the ground and whipping through the air, and Cris had no doubt that the appendages of the dismembered monsters could still crush a person to death if one was unlucky enough or stupid enough to get too close.

A chorus of cheers went up from both sides of the road, and Cris saw the "man" on the roof raise his right arm in what could have been a wave of acknowledgment. Then he lowered the arm until it was parallel with his left one, locked his wrists so that his palms were facing outward, and pointed both extremities down at the monsters again.

As Cris redirected his gaze toward the creatures' bodies, he heard a ringing in his ears for an instant. Then, to his utter amazement, what was left of the monsters began to shrink right before his eyes!

No . . . not shrink. He could see the stuff that comprised the insides of their bodies breaking up and flowing across the road, causing the outer skin to collapse as it did so. Although he couldn't feel any vibrations through the ground or through the air, it looked as if the things were being shaken apart, invisibly reduced to their smallest components.

"Sound waves," Tony surmised. "Can't hear a thing, but it's still music to my ears."

The spasmodic movement of the creatures' tentacles gradually slowed until only the tips were twitching. When all movement had ceased after about thirty seconds of the silent shock treatment, Cris looked back up toward the rooftop — just in time to see the cyborg turn and stride away out of sight. Another round of cheers went up, and this time Cris joined in, applauding vigorously as he kept his gaze fixed on the top of the building, hoping to catch another glimpse of the figure who, with seemingly little effort, had reduced two bug-creatures to shapeless piles of lifeless flesh. As he watched, he began to relish the thought of being able to do the same. . . .

Tony interrupted Cris's thoughts with a tap on his shoulder. "I think," he said, "that I've just decided what I want to be when I grow up."

"Me too," Cris said bitterly, so softly that not even his friend could sense the coldness in his tone.

It was . . . what? It was still supremely confident, but some other emotion — a foreign one — had entered Its consciousness. It had begun to wonder, to question whether Its plan was indeed perfect. The feeling was not at all pleasant. . . .

15

January 21-28, 2035

The official name of the facility was TA 04 S.21 — a short way of describing Cyborg Commando Secondary Base 1 (Manitowoc) attached to Primary Base 2 (Chicago) in Nation 4 (the United States) of the Trans-American Union. To those who lived and worked in the underground complex, it was known simply as "the base" — the only such place most of them had ever seen and, if the situation aboveground didn't improve, probably the last home they would ever know.

To Cris Holman, the place was mind-boggling — different from what he had expected in more ways than he could ever describe. It was a model of antiseptic, high-tech efficiency, an almost unbelievable contrast to the desolation and chaos of the outside world. He was all the more amazed when he found out that until just a short time ago, the facility in — or, more precisely, beneath — Manitowoc had been practically dormant.

He learned, in a necessarily brief indoctrination session, that it had been upgraded from a secondary base to "conditional primary" status just after the first of the bug-creatures had dropped from the sky. The primary base in Chicago was abandoned when that city was, as the army put it, "depopulated." Surviving personnel and still-functional equipment from that base had been transferred to Manitowoc, then combined with the people, supplies, and machinery already located at the latter site. Within a matter of days, the Manitowoc base was fully operational — a tribute to technology, foresight, and most of all human determination.

For the first few days after he arrived at the base, Cris was kept busy through all of his waking hours. He attended lectures and was subjected to a protracted and seemingly repetitious battery of physical, psychological, and intellectual examinations. He had practically no time to himself, and when he thought about that he was grateful, because the hectic schedule kept him from getting mired in grief and self-pity. The nights were the hardest times in that respect. In the few minutes after he lay down and before he fell asleep, Cris couldn't keep from thinking about all the people he had known who had died — Sara, Maura, his parents, even Bettser, who, for all his faults, didn't deserve what he had suffered. He tried to turn those feelings into something positive by using them as leverage to strengthen his resolve to get through the Cyborg Commando testing. But still, more often than not, he would wake up trembling at least once a night and have to shake off the effects of a horrible dream before he could get back to sleep.

Cris and the other candidates in his group were spared the complete medical and procedural details of how Cyborg Commandos were created. In fact, they were told scarcely more about the process than what Cris and Tony had learned from the lecture/demonstration they both had attended at the college several months earlier. What it boiled down to was this: anyone who passed through the preliminary testing would be asked to tape-record a statement of consent, declaring his willingness to go through final testing and, if he qualified, to be the subject of a "cybernetic implantation procedure" — fancy jargon for a brain transplant.

The officer who told Cris's group about the procedure was quick to emphasize that the operation was painless, and that subjects were in no way being asked to give up their lives. When a man's brain was removed, his body would be simultaneously hooked into a life-support and preservation system and then placed in cryogenic storage to await the day when the cyborg's term of service could be reunited. (It was mentioned, but certainly not emphasized, that the process of reversing the transplant had not yet been perfected.) The brain, in the meantime, would remain whole and healthy, and all of a subject's memories, psychological traits, and intellectual skills would be accessible and unaltered.

Each subject's brain would be housed inside a completely self-sufficient life-support capsule, and the capsule placed inside the best body that modern technology could fabricate. The brain would be connected by means of a computer interface to all of the body's electrical and mechanical systems. Every Cyborg Commando had "sensory input devices" that far exceeded the capability and sensitivity of the human eye, ear, nose, and taste buds; synthetic skeletal and muscular systems that were stronger and more durable than those of any man ever born; a "skin" that was impervious to abrasion and impact damage that would incapacitate a normal man; and — best of all, considering the circumstances — an array of built-in weaponry and defense mechanisms that turned the Cyborg Commando from an electromechanical super-human into an electromechanical super-human fighting machine.

For seven days, Cris and Tony were inseparable. They sat beside each other during meals, lectures, and testing. They lined up one after the other when the tests were of a solitary nature, as were most of the psychological and physical examinations. They slept in adjoining cots. Cris enjoyed Tony's company — his infectious enthusiasm at the prospect of "killing bugs," his unflagging optimism that both of them would make it through the program, and his willingness to console and encourage Cris when the past came trickling back into his memory and he needed some sympathy.

It was at one of those times that Cris learned the only personal facts that Tony had ever revealed to his friend. "The reason I have sympathy to give you," Tony had explained, "is because I haven't used any on myself." He went on to say that he hadn't had a real family since he was eight, when his parents had died in an airliner crash.

Because he had no other close relatives, for the next ten years he lived with an aunt and uncle who never grew attached to him and, on the day he left for college, made it unmistakably clear that they didn't expect or want to see him again. His "pseudoparents," as Tony called them, moved around a lot, preventing Tony from forming any lasting friendships while he was growing up. "You're the first person I've cared about since my mother and father died," Tony told Cris quietly one night.

The "Minelli therapy," as Tony referred to it in his more jocular moments, actually seemed to be doing Cris a lot of good. As their first week in the complex drew to a close, Cris thought back and realized how much his frame of mind had improved and stabilized. He still thought about the tragedies of his recent past, but he had been able to work out much of his sadness, and he had become geared toward vengeance rather than grief. He wanted not only to survive, but to succeed — to succeed in helping to obliterate the unearthly monsters that seemed intent on exterminating the human race.

The realization of his changed attitude hit Cris hard as he lay in bed on the night of Day Seven, and he wanted to express his feelings to Tony right then and there, but the sound of deep breathing from the adjacent bed told him that his friend was already fast asleep. That was okay; what Cris had to say to him could wait until the next morning. Cris rolled over, shut his eyes, and for the first time all week slept through the night.

*   *   *

The alarm sounded as usual. Cris, Tony, and the four other men who shared their sleeping quarters stumbled out of bed, freshened up, struggled into their coveralls, and started to go to breakfast, just as they had done every morning since checking in. Outside the door, the routine changed.

Cris was accosted by a pair of soldiers, one of whom said curtly but politely, "Come with us."

"What? Why?" Cris mumbled, still a little groggy from sleep.

"Where are you taking him?" Tony hollered.

"He'll be back," said the other soldier. "The rest of you head for the mess hall."

Cris, his thoughts a mixture of hope and fear because he didn't know what to expect, was led through a maze of corridors to a part of the base he had never visited before. The three men came to a closed door. One of the guards knocked briskly, opened the door without waiting for a response, and gestured for Cris to go inside.

The room contained only a small desk and two chairs. A man in a technician's white coat was seated at the desk. The only items on the desk were a single sheet of printed paper and a small, portable tape recorder. As the reality of the situation began to dawn on Cris, the man at the desk said, "Good morning," and motioned for him to take the other chair.

Cris seated himself facing the technician. He was about to start blurting out a string of questions when the man spoke.

"At this time," he began in a monotone, "the other members of your test group are being informed that they are unfit for recruitment into the Cyborg Commando Force. My purpose in being here is to inform you that you have qualified to enter final testing, and to request your consent for your participation in the program to continue."

The man's toneless delivery made it difficult for Cris to get overly excited about what he had just been told, but he was flabbergasted nevertheless. "I . . . I . . ." he stammered.

The technician cut him off before he could verbalize a coherent thought. "Please listen quietly and answer only when you are requested to do so. This conversation is being recorded, and the substance of it will be used as part of your final testing, should you choose to continue."

Cris kept quiet, stiffened in his chair, and forced himself to concentrate on every word.

He was asked if he understood the significance and the privilege of being selected to go through final testing; if he appreciated the dangers and the opportunities of allowing himself to be subjected to the implantation process; if he was prepared to commit himself completely and without reservation to his success as a Cyborg Commando and to the preservation and advancement of the Cyborg Commando Force. To each of those questions he answered with a soft but firm "Yes."

He was asked if he knew of any reason, heretofore undisclosed, why he should not be admitted into final testing; if he would be reluctant to undertake any task required of him; if he had any personal attachments that would cause him to regret becoming a Cyborg Commando. To each of those questions he gave a determined "No" — although, thinking of Tony, he paused for a heartbeat before answering the third one.

Finally, the technician administered what sounded like an oath, as Cris echoed it in "repeat after me" fashion:

"I, Cris Holman, an independent adult and a citizen of the United States of America, hereby give my unqualified consent for admission into the final examination phase of the Cyborg Commando program. I understand that if I am not disqualified during final testing, this consent extends to allowing myself to be subjected to the cybernetic implantation procedure. If I become a Cyborg Commando, I swear to use all the resources and capabilities of the cybernetic body at my disposal to the best of my ability, and as directed by any reasonable order issued by my superiors. I understand that failure to comply with the spirit as well as the letter of this promise shall render me subject to any penalties and punishments deemed appropriate."

Just as Cris uttered that last word, the man reached out and shut off the recorder. "That's it, son," he said with sudden warmth, extending his hand. "Congratulations."

For the rest of the day Cris was shuttled from room to room. Everything he did, even the short walks from one chamber to another, was preserved for posterity on a videocorder. At first being the absolute center of attention was disconcerting and even irritating, but he got accustomed to the everpresent camera and even succeeded in forgetting about it a few times. He was put through a series of tests that were, outwardly at least, essentially similar to the examinations he had undergone for the past week. He quickly learned that asking questions was useless, because either the people didn't respond at all or gave him answers that told him nothing he didn't already know. Since most of the tests were physical in nature, he soon resigned himself to being a glorified laboratory animal — and not a very glorified one at that.

He was allowed to rejoin the rest of his test group for dinner that evening — the first meal he had been given all day. He entered the mess hall to a hearty but somewhat strained round of applause. He spotted Tony — hard to miss, since he had climbed up on a table and was yelling with reckless abandon — and went straight to him.

Tony hopped down and they embraced. When Cris pulled away a few seconds later, he looked into a wide smile and a pair of eyes moistening with tears. "Well," Tony said, his voice quavering, "one of us made it."

"I'm sorry," Cris said softly, his happiness submerged beneath his concern for his friend. "What went wrong? Why didn't they take you too?"

"My brain's just fine," he said, tapping his temple. "It's my body that's the problem. It seems I have the sort of carcass that might not take well to being stuck in a deep freeze for who knows how long. I told 'em I'd be willing to give it a shot anyway, but once these military types make up their minds there's no reasoning with them."

"So what happens to you now?" asked Cris, suddenly afraid that their short but strong friendship might be coming to an end.

"I get to stay here," Tony said. "Because I have such an appealing personality, they're going to train me for a job in the physical examination area. I get to give tests instead of take them. The bad news is that all of my patients will be men."

"A disappointment that I'm sure you'll find a way to overcome," countered Cris as relief and happiness washed over him. "We will get to stay in touch then, I presume."

"Yeah, I guess so, but I don't think we're going to see each other for quite a while. You're a hot property now, my boy, and I'm just a plain old working stiff."

"Not to me, Tony. Not to me."

They sat and ate together, filling the time between bites with small talk. When mealtime was over, a soldier appeared beside Cris's chair to escort him to his new quarters. "Let me spend one more night with my friend," Cris said, trying to sound insistent but knowing what the result of his request would be.

"You'll see me again," said Tony. "Maybe sooner, maybe later, but you'll see me again. You can count on it."

"Good—"

"So long, Cris. Just say so long."

16

January 31, 2035

The first thing Cris saw when he woke up was a stranger.

"Good morning, P-17. Welcome back."

Now he was really confused. Who was this man? Why was he calling him "Pee seventeen"? Where was he being welcomed back from?

"What's going on?" Cris mumbled, trying to inject a note of sharpness into the question even though he was still fighting the grogginess of his half-awake state.

"Take a couple of minutes to get your bearings, and then I'll tell you what you need to know."

Cris flexed and relaxed his muscles a few times, working from his arms to his abdomen to his legs and back up again. He blinked his eyes rapidly a few times, trying to open them wider each time. He was calmly amazed, and pleasantly surprised, to discover that in the space of just two minutes, his disorientation had disappeared. He felt more alert, healthier, than he could remember ever having felt before. He sat up briskly, not bothering to use his arms to pull his upper body to a vertical position, and had to restrain the urge to bounce up off the bunk and start doing some vigorous calisthenics. He was . . . energized!

"How do you feel?"

"Fine . . . I think," Cris replied. "But this is not the way I usually feel right when I wake up. I'm a real zombie in the morning — just ask my . . . " He stopped himself, suddenly aware that he was rambling and self-conscious because this man obviously didn't care about the last ninety percent of his elaborate answer. And he had almost mentioned his mother — something that embarrassed him and saddened him at the same time, as visions of his long-gone home life flashed unbidden through his mind.

"My name is Traynor," the man said, breaking the brief but awkward silence. I'm here to tell you what you've been through, and a little bit about what's going to happen next."

"What do you mean, what I've been through? I went to sleep last night, and today you woke me up, and . . ." Suddenly, Cris remembered. "The final testing! Did I pass?"

"Actually, you've been 'asleep' for three days,"

the man said. "As for passing the final test, there was really not much question of that. If you hadn't all but made it through, we never would have put you under."

"Wait a minute," Cris interrupted. "How come nobody told me I passed?" A flood of conflicting emotions washed over him — happiness at finding out he had made it through, frustration at having information withheld from him, and anger that his moment of triumph was being spoiled by that same frustration.

"Try to stay calm," Traynor said, with the air of someone who had been through this sort of conversation before. "I know it's an old excuse, and in most cases it's just that — an excuse. But there were some things we simply couldn't tell you before we prepped you."

Cris took a deep breath, consciously tried to relax his mind and his muscles with moderate success, and leaned forward on the edge of his bunk. "All right. I'm listening. And this time, don't leave anything out."

"Before you went to sleep three nights ago," Traynor began, "we already knew that your brain had passed all the tests. The organ itself is in perfect health, or at least as close to that as anyone's we've ever examined. Despite what you went through just before you joined the program, you're also psychologically sound. You have some aggressive tendencies that seem to have developed only recently, no doubt caused by your desire to avenge the death of your loved ones. But aggression is not an undesirable quality, as long as it remains channeled along productive lines — certainly preferable to indecisiveness and insecurity, especially considering the line of work you're about to engage in."

"All nice to know," said Cris, trying to keep his pride and excitement under control. "But why couldn't you tell me all that before you knocked me out?"

"The final test didn't involve your brain at all — it had to do with the rest of you. You did fine on all the preliminary physical examinations; strong heart, clean lungs, above-average muscle tone, and so forth. But we have one policy here that no candidate ever finds out about until after the fact. To put it simply, we won't use your brain unless we're sure you'll have a body to go back to. A body that's placed in stasis is very vulnerable. For instance, muscles and organs that aren't in perfect condition will atrophy. Because we haven't learned how to perfectly simulate the activity of the lymphatic system, we have to be sure that a body is absolutely free of viruses and minor physical traumas before we place it into a life-support capsule. So, for the last three days, your body has undergone the most intensive examination that modern technology can provide.

"If you'll forgive the mechanical analogy, we

needed to be sure that you were in perfect working order. We had to subject your body to a lot of stress, and we had to keep you unconscious so that your brain wouldn't interfere with what we were asking your body to do. We gave you several types of examinations to find out how your systems would respond if extraordinary demands were placed upon them.

"The process is similar to testing an engine," Traynor continued without meaning to be condescending. "It's easy to just start it up and see if it runs, but to really test it you've got to push it to the limit. If it runs smoothly under extreme conditions, conditions that are far more adverse than what it's normally expected to endure, then you've got a good engine. If we had discovered even one small chronic imperfection in your physiological profile — any trace of disease, any congenital condition that wouldn't have showed up in a general examination — then we would have dropped you."

"So I ran well, did I?" Cris asked, then immediately followed that rhetorical question with a real one. "If you put me through my paces, and then some, how come I don't feel stiff and sore, or even tired? In fact—"

"In fact, you feel as though you could run ten miles with a piano on your back and not even break a sweat," said Traynor. "That's because in the last phase of the testing, we pumped you full of nutrients and natural stimulants to offset the effects of all the stress and exertion your body had been put through. You're full of energy right now, but it won't last. Your metabolism has been super-accelerated, but only temporarily. Your body is assimilating those nutrients almost as fast as we introduced them into it. By the time this conversation is over, your system will be back to normal, and your stomach will be sending strong signals to your brain to do something about getting a real meal for the first time in three days."

"Fine and dandy," said Cris. "But right now the only thing I'm hungry for is more information. I still don't understand why, if what you're after is my brain, it was so important for my body to pass all these tests. I went into this with my eyes open. They told me — they told all of us — that the operation was a one-way deal. Once I go through with this, I don't ever expect to have my brain put back in my real body." Cris paused after he made that last remark, remembering that Tony had said essentially the same thing but had been rejected anyway.

"Yes, you do — or, at least, you will," Traynor explained patiently. "Maybe right now you don't care, or you've convinced yourself that you don't. But we know from experience — even what little experience we've had — that once the transfer is accomplished, there's a part of your psyche that's going to feel . . . incomplete. We can't keep you from having that feeling, but we can do our best to guarantee that when — and I do mean *when* — we develop a way to reverse the process, your body will be ready and waiting for you. From that day forward, no one will be forced to remain in a cybernetic body any longer than he or she wants to. For now, we can't offer you that promise, so we try to soften the psychological trauma the best way we can."

"I still say there isn't going to be any psychological trauma in this case," Cris said, feeling some apprehension but doing his best to conceal it beneath a veneer of confidence. "You guys went to a lot of trouble for nothing. If you had told me all of this three days ago, I could have told you not to worry. . . ." He stopped, disconcerted despite himself as he caught the thin, almost patronizing smile that flashed across the other man's face. "Okay," he continued, recalling a question that had been in the back of his mind ever since he woke up, "answer me this, Doc. Why did you call me 'Pee seventeen' when you woke me up, and why haven't you used my real name once through this whole conversation?"

"First of all," said Traynor, "I'm not a doctor — not a medical doctor, at any rate. I'm a technician — I interpret and analyze test results, but I don't actually perform the tests. And I suppose it won't surprise you to know that I also have some experience in psychology. Second of all, I don't know your real name — it's none of my business. Your designation from this point forward, until such time as your brain is reunited with your body, is P-17 — the seventeenth unit in the P series."

"So instead of a name, I now have a serial number. Just what I've always wanted."

"I think I know how you feel," the man said, careful to stress the first two words of the sentence. "But there's a reason for us not using your real name from now on — again, a reason you might not fully appreciate until . . . later. We think it's important to establish separate identities for you — the real you — and the 'you' that will be occupying a cybernetic body. As Commando P-17, you will have all the memories, all the psychological traits that are in your mind right now, so that in the technical, scientific sense, 'you' will not have changed a bit. We will be able to predict, with a reasonable degree of success, how you will react and respond to different situations, based on the psychological testing you've already undergone." Traynor paused a beat, to emphasize what was coming, but not long enough to give Cris a chance to interrupt.

"But no one — not us, and certainly not you — must ever lose sight of the fact that your true identity is not as a cybernetic soldier, but as a human being. If we didn't think this was important, we would continue to call you by your given name — and we might not care about keeping your body ready to come back to.

"Besides," he continued, leaning back and smiling, "this makes it a lot easier for the clerical staff. If two brains named John Smith were put into two identical bodies, how would we ever tell them apart?"

"You're the technician, Doc," said Cris, picking up on the joke. "I've got enough problems of my own already. First and foremost, what does a *man* have to do to get something to eat around here?"

*   *   *

After a rather unspectacular breakfast, which Cris tried hard not to think of as the standard condemned man's last meal, he was given another briefing by another man he had never seen before.

This conversation — more properly, a monologue by the other man — took place in a room similar to others Cris had been in during his testing. It looked like an ordinary room, but he was pretty sure it contained the same kinds of hidden cameras and microphones that had been monitoring him. The chair to which he had been directed was comfortable enough, but it was fastened to the floor and molded so that he could only sit in one position — a position, he supposed, that enabled built-in sensors in the chair to keep constant track of his pulse rate, body temperature, respiration, perspiration rate, and who knew how many other things.

Cris had become accustomed to being monitored, prodded, and probed either electronically or physically, and he had long ago stopped worrying about what the scientists and doctors might be finding out about him when he was being examined. What the hell, he thought, I can't change my blood pressure from one minute to the next and I can't control how much I sweat or don't sweat. So, what you see on your output devices is what you get — take me or leave me.

Cris started to project his aggression toward the short, gray-haired man who sat across the room from him (on an ordinary plastic chair that he could move wherever he wanted!), but quickly decided otherwise — just in case they had a way of knowing what he was thinking.

"You're a bit agitated," the man began in a flat, utterly clinical tone of voice. For an instant, Cris wondered how he could know that. He was being careful not to fidget, he was purposely keeping his breathing slow and regular. He was doing everything he could to appear calm and relaxed. "That's not unusual," the man continued, "so it's better, if you don't try to fight it or conceal it. In fact, if you weren't somewhat excited right now, with six hours left before surgery, I think we'd have second thoughts about you."

"Six hours?! Is that all the time I have? I thought—"

"What you were told was that if you qualified,

the implantation would take place with all due speed thereafter. I'm sorry if you expected more time, but you must realize by now that we don't have any time to waste."

For the next half-hour or so, Cris sat quietly while the nameless scientist droned out a general but still technical explanation of how the transfer process worked. He didn't care much about the specifics and all he could seem to think about was the little bit of time he had left — perhaps his last few hours ever as a living, breathing, *real* human being. Besides, the man's delivery and tone of voice were not exactly designed to keep a listener on the edge of his sculptured couch.

When the man had gone through everything he was obliged to recite, without stopping any longer than necessary to take a breath now and then, he abruptly cleared his throat and stood up. The combination was sufficient to bring Cris out of his half-dazed state, and he paid close attention to the man's last few sentences.

"You haven't consciously retained much, if any, of what I've just told you." The tone, as before, was matter-of-fact, practically lifeless. "Again, that's not unusual. But the key word there is 'consciously' — you have, subconsciously, taken in everything I've said, and the understanding of it that you have achieved on that level will enable you to perceive what happens to you during the later stages of the process. You will find that helpful," the man said, and for the first time a thin smile broke the monotony of his expression.

"What now?" Cris asked, unwilling and unable to phrase a more specific question.

The man lapsed back into his droning lecture-voice. "I was about to tell you about the last phase of the pre-operation procedure. When I leave and shut the door behind me, the room will begin to fill with an odorless anesthetic gas. A short time later, you will be in an extremely deep sleep — not comatose, but very close to it. This period of sensory deprivation is necessary because we need to take final readings of your brain structure, and then we need a few hours to make the last adjustments to your personal interface. During that time your brain must remain identical to the configuration it was in when we took our final readings. If we allowed your brain to accumulate memories and sensory input right up until the moment the operation begins . . . well, let's just say we might end up with some wires dangling."

"And how many wires did you let dangle before you figured that out?" Cris shot at him, figuring he had nothing to lose by being sarcastic at this point.

"Only a few," the man responded calmly, doing his best to put on a reassuring smile as he rose and turned toward the door. "Only a few."

"Thanks a lot for the confidence booster," Cris retorted.

The man did not react. He opened the door,

stepped through it, turned to face Cris, bowed his head ever so slightly, and said, "Good luck to you."

Then he closed the door, and Cris was alone with his thoughts.

Five minutes later, when his lungs had filled with anesthetic gas, he was simply alone.

17

January 31, 2035

It had been a long day and Nora was tired. But she knew there was one more transplant scheduled to begin before midnight, and she had decided to stick around at the research center instead of going to her apartment in another section of the complex. She felt as though she was personally involved in each of these brave recruits' lives — and she made a point of going over each of their files before the surgical process was under way.

She walked into her office bathroom and pulled a drinking glass off a shelf above the sink. She turned on the tap and let the water run for a few minutes before filling the glass. She gulped down the contents within a few seconds and stuck the container back under the faucet for a refill. Then she turned off the water and, glass in hand, walked back out to her desk.

It had been almost three weeks since she had drunk anything stronger than soda, and it was all she could do to keep from pulling out the bottle of scotch she knew was locked in one of the drawers of her file cabinet. "I should have thrown the damn thing out," she cursed softly, and then took another drink of water.

She picked up the folder that her secretary had laid in the middle of her desk. The cover was blank except for a letter-number combination handwritten in the corner.

The system for "naming" Cyborg Commando units was simple, a variant of the way the military designated different models of aircraft, ships, and ground vehicles. The earliest models were the "A" series. Each of them was numbered sequentially — A-1, A-2, and so on. Whenever technicians made a significant change or improvement in the cybernetic body, the numbering would start over with the next letter in the alphabet used as a prefix. Nora didn't have access to records from all the CC bases around the world, but as far as she knew, there were very few "A" or "B" units. That left John Edwards, unit C-12, pretty high on the seniority list.

"I wonder what we'll do when we get to the end of the alphabet," Nora mused cynically. "Only ten letters left after this one."

She sighed and took another drink of water,

then sat back in her seat and rested the folder in her lap. The last two and a half weeks had been rough. When she learned about the invasion and realized what it meant for the Cyborg Commando program, she had thrown herself into her work with a vigor she had not felt for years. At the same time she vowed to overcome her addiction to alcohol — a vow she had not broken, but which was being severely tested.

Nora had kept her resolve strong by reminding herself that her struggle against her habit was nothing compared to what most of the people on Earth were going through. In the underground complex she was reasonably safe; for that she was grateful. But the privilege of relative safety was attached to a responsibility, and that was where her job came in. This base, and others like it, were the only hope anyone left on the face of the earth had of ever leading a normal life again.

Whatever they were, the horrible creatures that had invaded seemed to be bent on wiping every last man, woman, and child off the face of the planet. Nora remembered having seen a laughable classic science-fiction screen treatment of an invasion similar to the real one going on outside the complex. The movie, she recalled, was titled "Planet in Peril," and she doubted anyone alive today would still call it laughable.

No man alive could defeat the monsters that now ravaged the world, but the Cyborg Commando

— he was a different story. CCs were battling the creatures to a standstill, or better, whenever they had encountered one another, but the super-soldiers were terribly outnumbered by the monsters. The gloomiest estimates Nora had heard put the ratio at about 100,000 to 1, but the optimistic ones weren't much better.

To make matters worse, Nora and her colleagues had been instructed to assume that at least half of the active CCs around the world had been destroyed in the first surge of the invasion — which made their work that much more critical. If enough men could be transformed into cyborgs quickly enough . . . well, it was a long shot, but it was the only one.

The only problems, and they were big ones, were the amount of time it took to create a cybernetic soldier and the large numbers of volunteers needed. Many of those who had been approached, civilians and soldiers alike, said they would rather "stay human" and take their chances against the deadly creatures instead of risking death in the operating room, or possibly suffering eventual insanity because their brains could not be reunited with their bodies.

"Can't really blame them," Nora sighed as she opened the file now resting on her lap — the records of a man who was about to become Cyborg Commando P-17. What she saw inside made her gasp, then cry out loudly. Letting the folder fall to the floor, she sprang from her chair and raced out of her office.

*   *   *

When Nora came to, the first figure she saw was the Cyborg Commando she would always know as John Edwards.

"So, do you want to tell me about it, or should I guess?" The part of C-12 that still was — and always would be — a compassionate human being spoke through his voice synthesizer. Nora said nothing for a few minutes, still trying to sort out exactly what had happened to her.

"How long was I out?" she asked finally.

"About fifteen minutes." C-12 sat down on the end of the bed and waited for her to speak again.

Nora looked at the Cyborg Commando, who was not only one of the best friends she had ever known, but also someone for whom she had developed a great deal of affection. She would have liked to see the whole John Edwards sitting at the end of her hospital bed. But the only part of him with her now was his brain, and brains couldn't put their arms around you and hold you when you needed it.

She sighed and pushed a few errant strands of hair back off her face. Maybe it was best that C-12, and not the human John Edwards, was here with her now. She had come to love the part of C-12 that was also part of John, but if he had still been in his human body, she would have wanted him as her lifemate, and there were too many years between them for the two of them to consider a serious relationship.

Maybe if they had grown up and met in the mid-1990s, when moral values were much more liberal just after the discovery of the AIDS vaccine, they might have had a chance. But the pendulum had swung back the other way by the time they met three years ago. In the social climate of the time, lifemates more than ten or fifteen years apart in age were, to put it graciously, frowned upon.

Nora sighed again and then, suddenly, she remembered the last thing she saw before blacking out.

"Is P-17 doing all right so far?" she asked, fighting to keep the shakiness and apprehension she felt from showing in her voice.

"I don't know. I was too busy picking you up off the floor to pay much attention to what was going on around me. Are you all right now?" John asked, the concern evident in his tone.

"Yes, I think so. But I have to know how it's going down there. I have to get back—"

"You're not going anywhere for at least a few minutes, until I'm sure you're not going to hit the ground again when you stand up. Not that I mind carrying you around in my arms, but I wouldn't want that brilliant mind — or any other interesting part of you — to suffer any damage in a fall. Besides, they won't let you back in on this one. You've been diagnosed as exhausted, stressful, and, uh . . ."

"Alcoholic, right?" she asked, her tone implying resignation rather than annoyance.

"That theory was put forth," John said gently.

Nora's face felt uncomfortably hot, and she had to blink rapidly to keep the moisture that was forming in her eyes from running down her cheeks. "I have to know what's happening in there," she said, her tone almost pleading.

"Would you like me to check?" John asked. He thought he knew why she cared so much, but he was waiting for her to tell him.

"Yes, please hurry and let me know how he's doing!" Nora said, her sense of urgency growing stronger every minute. C-12 stood and walked to the door, leaving the room without another word.

To Nora it seemed like hours before he returned but in fact John was gone for less than fifteen minutes. When C-12 walked back into the room, Nora sat up straight in the bed and looked hard at him, fervently wishing that CCs had facial muscles so that she could read his expression.

"Well?" she asked impatiently, anxiously.

"P-17 is doing just fine," John said. "I spent about ten minutes in the observation booth — enough time to pick up on some very positive comments being made by some members of the surgi-

cal team. They say he's one of the best candidates
they've had in a long time, and they have no concern about the outcome of this procedure."

He gave her that information in as gentle and
hopeful a tone of voice as his electronic larynx
would allow. Then he added, a hint of the old John
Edwards cockiness returning, "In fact, someone
said — and I heard it — that he is the best specimen they've had since they had the privilege —
well, maybe they didn't use the word 'privilege', but
I'm sure that's what they were thinking — of having
operated on none other than—"

"C-12, right?"

"Right! How'd ya guess? Boy, are you percep-
tive!" John feigned surprise, although, again, this
was one of those times when it would have added
a lot if she could have seen his face.

Nora grinned.

"It's nice to see you smiling, although I have to
admit, I'm just a wee bit envious," John said, and
then added, "Do you know how frustrating it is to
feel like your nose itches so bad you could scream
when you don't even have a nose you can
scratch? Have you experts ever figured out a way
to rid us poor tin men of some of these mini-trau-
mas we have to live through, day in and day out?"

Nora stopped smiling, and John was sorry he'd
used the word "trauma." His visual sensors saw
the change of expression on her face, and he
wished he had eyes so he could show her with a

look the sympathy and love he was feeling for her at this moment. "Nora, don't worry," he said as gently as he could. "Your son will be all right."

Nora's jaw dropped slightly, and she just stared at the half-human, half-mechanical man standing beside her bed. Then, when she was able, she asked in a feeble tone, "How did you know?"

John Edwards sat back down on the bed and rested his hand on Nora's foot, a gesture he hoped would be soothing — at least emotionally. "I saw the look on your face when you came into the observation room as they were removing the brain. You screamed 'Cris!' and then passed out cold. I figured he had to be someone very close to you. Since the only person from your past you've ever told me about was your child, and since the age was about right, I just guessed from there. For your sake, I'm sorry I was right."

Nora lay back down, calmer now that she had accepted the fact that John knew her secret.

"Do you want to talk about it?" John asked her softly.

"Yes. As long as I can do that in the observation booth. I want to watch," she said decisively.

"Do you think that's a good idea?" John asked.

"For once in his life, I'm going to be there for him," Nora said, the look of determination in her eyes leaving no doubt in John's mind that this was something she would not be talked out of.

"Okay. But do you feel all right?"

"I'm fine," she said, slowly swinging her feet over the side of the bed and indicating that she was not all that fine by her rather unsteady return to her feet.

"In that case, slip your arm through mine, and I'll escort you there. And they say we CCs aren't chivalrous!" John teased, offering her his arm.

"Your artillery isn't turned on, is it?" Nora asked a little hesitantly.

"No, but believe it or not, I am. Are you sure you removed—"

"We removed everything from the skull on down," she said before he had a chance to finish his question.

"It was just a thought." He would have shrugged his shoulders, if he had any.

John insisted that Nora use the wheelchair that had been left for her outside the door of her room. She protested, mildly, but decided it would take much less time if she gave in than if they argued about it. He could be very stubborn where her well-being was concerned, she thought, with no small amount of appreciation.

John pushed the chair, with Nora in it, a short distance through a couple of corridors and up the ramp leading to the observation deck. Once inside, he pushed the chair up against the window, so she could get a good overview.

What she saw when she looked into the room below made her gasp and shudder visibly.

She had rarely noticed the human side — or inhuman side, as this seemed — of the cybernetic surgical procedure. But now, looking down at the dormant body of her only child, she wanted to scream. What had possessed the boy to volunteer for this? Why hadn't his father tried to stop him? How soon would they have the technology to reverse the brain transplant so she could see and love her son as a normal human being? These questions, and others, ran rapidly through her consciousness.

Nora forced herself to take a long look at the inert body lying nude on the operating table. It would be put in cryogenic storage in a very short while, and she wanted — needed — to get a good look at the son she hadn't seen since infancy.

She was proud of the strong, muscular young man Cris appeared to have become. His frame was very much like his father's, she noted, but he seemed in much better physical condition than she could remember Marc Holman being as a young man.

She decided her former husband must be dead. She couldn't imagine the Marc Holman she used to know letting his son volunteer to be a guinea pig for any cause. Either Marc is dead, or Cris is his mother's child and will do what he pleases no matter who says he can't, Nora thought sadly. . . .

"This is absolute insanity! It's ridiculous!" A voice from the past entered Nora's thoughts. She vividly recalled the day Marc Holman had spoken those words. It was the day she had told him that she had a chance to turn all her effort and knowledge toward the development of a super-human soldier — a chance she didn't intend to pass up. She would never forget the terrible fight that had followed.

"Marc, I'll only be gone for six months, during the very earliest stages of development. We can hire someone to watch Cris while you're working, and—"

"And how do I explain your absence to a two-month-old baby?" Marc interrupted, the anger and hurt evident in his tone.

"Marc, you know how much I love Cris, but I know he'll be all right with you, and I'll drive home once a month to see you both. This isn't about him. You're angry because of what I want to do. I know how you feel about using human—"

Her husband didn't allow her to finish. "Look, you know I wouldn't want to keep you from furthering your career, but this cyborg nonsense is just that — nonsense! And even worse, it's murder!"

"Marc, I wish you would just try to understand. I believe in this project. I wish you could see what this could mean to our defense program. And I've been asked to get in on the ground floor. I could learn more from this and earn more recognition than I ever dreamed of at this stage in my life!"

Marc Holman had refused to further discuss the

subject. "You are a brilliant psychologist who's already recognized for what you are, or you wouldn't even have been asked to participate in this travesty. You can build on what you already have without leaving home. And if you choose to leave and do this thing, then don't bother to come back — ever!"

At that Marc had walked away, and Nora stood, more hurt than anything, looking after the man who had once vowed to support her goals and her dreams, just as she had promised to support his.

The next day she officially accepted the offer to participate in the cyborg research program. Not out of defiance. Not out of anger. She really did believe in the program, and she was still hopeful that Marc would come to his senses. She knew he couldn't have meant what he said when he had told her not to bother to return.

But he had.

She phoned home every night, but he refused to look at her or talk to her. She drove home every couple of weekends for the first several months, but he wouldn't let her in the house. And he absolutely refused to let her see Cris. "You deserted him!" he had shouted at her once through the locked front door of their home, while she stood outside pleading with him to be reasonable.

After six months the team of scientists developing the Cyborg Commando technology had made great strides, and even loftier accomplishments seemed to be in store. She was offered a promotion and chose to take it. It was then she decided to file for divorce and ask for custody of her son. She had no love left for Marc Holman, but she desperately missed Cris and wanted him near her.

After a bitter court battle, the judge awarded custody of Cris to "the parent who has remained with the child and cared for him since birth." The implication was clear: The judge agreed with Marc that Nora had "deserted" her child. And now she had lost him.

She was awarded visitation rights — at least that was better than not being able to see Cris at all — and had driven home twice a month for the next few months.

Those were the times she enjoyed most in life. Sometimes, while spending a weekend with her tiny son, she would wonder why she had ever wanted to pursue a career at all. During those wonderfully happy times she wanted nothing more from life than to be with him.

But then Marc Holman moved himself and his son halfway across the country, presumably so that he could accept a new position. Nora knew the move was intended to keep her from seeing her son. There was no way she could travel the distance on a regular basis unless she quit the cyborg program.

She considered quitting — quite seriously, in fact — but she couldn't tear herself away just then, when they were on the verge of performing the first brain transplant operation. . . .

"So I immersed myself in my work and tried to forget about Cris. In other words, I abandoned my son," she told John Edwards while the surgical team was installing her son's brain in its new body. And then she added, so softly that the words would have been inaudible to a human ear, "But I never stopped loving him."

John felt more love and compassion for this woman than he had ever felt for anyone in his life. And human or machine, his feelings for her could not be stronger than they were at this moment. "If your son is half the person his mother is, he'll not only make one hell of a Cyborg Commando, he'll also remain one hell of a human being," he said.

It took Nora a few minutes to respond, while she tried to keep control of her emotions. Finally she almost choked her response. "Thank you, John," she said with love in her eyes.

18

Cris Holman was aware. Aware of the fact that he was aware of . . . nothing.

He could feel, but had no way of touching. He could see, but had no way of looking. He could hear — but how can someone listen to absolute, utter silence?

I . . . AM.

Those two words are the only way to describe the first complete, conscious thought that had originated in Cris Holman's brain since the cybernetic implantation procedure had begun. Two words that conveyed the most important piece of information any human being — any human brain — could possess. Cris was *alive*. He didn't know how, and he didn't know for how long, but nothing else beyond the simple fact of his continued existence mattered at all right now.

I . . . AM . . . HERE. . . . WHERE . . . IS HERE?

Lacking any means by which to receive new information, his brain was incapable of answering the question his mind had posed. This did not dismay Cris. He didn't expect an answer, but he was satisfied with and gratified by his ability to ask the question.

Then, much more rapidly than he could keep track of them, thoughts and memories and sensations came flooding back, rushing to the surface of his consciousness, all of them competing with the others for his attention.

He could not organize his thoughts; he could not *do* anything with any of them, except to note their existence as each of them broke through the surface tension into his awareness and then, almost instantaneously, was pushed out of the way and back down by another emerging mental image.

Cris had no way of sensing the jubilation that filled the surgical chamber when this happened. His brain, which had been shut down almost to the point of total inactivity — death — before the extraction process began, was now operating, almost as well as ever, on its own specially designed life-support system and was in the process of being hooked up to an electronic, computer-assisted interface.

Although the detachment (from the body) and reattachment (to the interface) of the brain was not the most difficult part of the process for those performing the transfer, it was the most hazardous part for the brain — the person — on whom it was performed. Once the brain was deadened, speed was paramount. The surgical team had to detach it from the spinal cord, then connect each bundle of cranial nerves to one of the sockets in the interface, and then disconnect and reroute all of the smaller nerves that controlled the sensory organs located in the head.

Before, during, and after all of this was going on, other medical technicians ("doctors" is not quite an accurate word) were busy slicing through muscle tissue and cartilage to give the nerve specialists room to work; disconnecting, tying off, and reconnecting the ends of arteries and veins to make sure the brain had a continual supply of blood; and doing a seeming myriad of other small but crucial tasks to insure that the separation of brain from body, as shocking as it was to the human system, was accomplished with the least amount of trauma and the shortest delay possible.

The technological level of the microsurgery involved was as advanced over the medical procedures of the mid-twentieth century as those procedures were advanced over what doctors did for their patients in the Renaissance era, when drawing blood was the cure for practically any ailment, since (apparently) bleeding to death was considered preferable to dying of an illness. But still, with all their gadgetry and knowledge, the doctors of the early twenty-first century had one great obstacle to overcome: the physical and physiological limitations of the human brain itself. No one had yet figured out how to insure the survival of the brain under such conditions — not so long ago thought to be utterly fatal — for any longer than six hours.

And six hours is not a long time when tens of thousands of nerve endings, blood vessels, and muscle fibers all have to be attended to. Fortunately, how the severed nerve ends were tied off or reconnected was not of utmost importance. When a nerve bundle was fastened to an interface socket, for example, it made little difference in most cases which minuscule pathway was hooked into which microscopic receptacle. Later, the engineers could (and always did) fiddle with the circuitry that led from the interface to the mechanisms that each nerve-circuit was supposed to control — *had* to control, based on the makeup of Cris Holman's central nervous system. Their work guaranteed that when, for instance, Cris's brain wanted to move his body's left leg, his body's right arm wouldn't move instead.

At this point, Cris Holman's brain was far from

being able to order anything to move. It was a living organism, becoming more alive all the time if brain-wave activity was any indication (which was the cause for the short celebration in the surgical chamber), and it was conscious, in a manner of speaking. But right now it resembled nothing more than a fully charged battery with no way to use its power, the operating system of a computer that didn't have anything to operate.

I AM . . . CRIS. No — I AM . . . CRIS'S BRAIN. THAT IS . . . DIFFERENT.

With every passing second, Cris Holman — the part of him that was still sentient — became more capable of independent thought, more able to gather information and draw conclusions . . . more able to think. What he had to think *about* was still limited to the memories his brain had stored before he was anesthetized, but that limitation was really no limitation at all. The brain of any normal adult human being — and most abnormal ones — contains enough memories to last a lifetime, even if no new ones were ever thereafter introduced into the sensory/neural network.

Cris Holman did not feel deprived or deficient; he was senseless, but not thoughtless. He thought with a clarity he had never experienced before, since his mental processes were unhindered, undistracted by the sights and sounds and smells of the world around him. If he wanted to, he could send his thoughts scurrying along a line of complicated reasoning, discarding undesirable alternatives in a fraction of a millisecond and coming to a conclusion in less time than it takes a normal human being to scratch his nose.

If he wanted, he could focus on one thought, one concept, and examine it in his mind's eye with such thoroughness, such single-mindedness, that a second or so later he felt as though he had completely exhausted the subject — but if he thought about the same thing a second later, the process started all over again. He didn't forget, he just never got tired of remembering.

If he wanted, he could think anything, remember anything . . . do anything! In its conscious/unconscious/unfettered state, Cris Holman's brain had access to memories he had not thought about for years, if ever. He perceived connections between events, between ideas, that had never before occurred to him. He remembered things that had caused him pleasure (SARA'S FACE, MAURA, MOM AND DAD . . .) and things that had caused him sadness (SARA, MOM AND DAD, MAURA . . .).

Most vividly of all now, he remembered the words he had heard from the anonymous, monotonous man — the last human being who had put any memories into his brain. He waited for opportunities to verify what that man had told him would happen. So far, he had experienced none of the sensations he had been told to expect — the sensations the scientists could foresee. What he was sensing right now went deeper than those predictable phenomena, and he was quite willing to savor what he was going through for as long as it would last. He had an inexhaustible supply of mental energy, and practically as much patience.

I AM . . . APART. SOMETHING IS MISSING.

Was this the point at which Cris Holman's brain was finally separated from his body? Or was this simply the result of *thinking* about the separation of brain from body and imagining what it would feel like? In the instant after he phrased those questions to himself, Cris realized that both of them could be answered YES . . . and the answers didn't really matter anyway. He made up his mind not to concern himself with what was happening outside him, and to concentrate on what was happening inside him.

BUT . . . IT'S IMPOSSIBLE NOT TO THINK ABOUT SOMETHING . . . BECAUSE YOU HAVE TO THINK ABOUT IT IN ORDER TO NOT THINK ABOUT IT.

He was amused by the paradox.

IF I COULD SMILE, I WOULD. BUT EVEN THOUGH I CAN'T, I CAN.

Cris Holman had no way of knowing if his instincts were accurate. Indeed, he had no way of knowing where instinct began and ended because, in his present state, any thought — all thought — was instinctual. But his perception was correct. The cranium of his body had been opened, his brain had been loosened from the protecting and nourishing membranes that surrounded it, and, just as he was feeling his sensations of separateness, Cris Holman's operating system was lifted, ever so gently, out of the space it had occupied for almost twenty years.

It was moved, with utmost care, a distance of three feet through the antiseptic air of the surgical chamber and nestled in a plastic shell that had been specially molded to accommodate the former contents of Cris Holman's skull. No two of these capsules were identical, because, of course, no two brains are precisely the same in size, shape, and volume. The cybernetic body into which this capsule would be placed was not unique; any brain could function within it and operate it if it was connected properly. But the cranial capsule itself was as much a part of Cris, as essential to his continued existence, as the brain that resided inside it.

ONE AGAIN. BACK WHERE I BELONG.

The feeling of separation was not disturbing or even really disconcerting, but Cris was glad that it had passed nonetheless. He felt somehow better, more comfortable, more purposeful, when he could sense that his brain was not vulnerable. He still had nothing to do but think, and he still relished this feeling, but underlying all of his thoughts now was the impression, the assumption, that soon his brain once again would have other functions to perform.

I AM . . . CONNECTED. TO WHAT?

With methodical precision, for now there was no need to hurry, the electrotechnicians had gone to work. Using a combination of applied knowledge and systematic testing — a fancy euphemism for a procedure just a couple of degrees more sophisticated than trial and error — they would examine each of the leads that came out of the electromechanical end (as opposed to the organic end) of the interface.

Once they had identified each nerve in terms of its general function, they could connect the lead to either a single wire or a switching circuit that married that nerve to two other wires. One of these two wires (or the single one, when only one connection was necessary) led to an inboard computer contained within the brain capsule — an electronic brain designed to augment the organic one, to operate life support and other internal systems, and to take over monitoring and maintenance of other essential systems when the cyborg's organic brain becomes unconscious or incapacitated.

The other lead in a two-wire system went directly from the organic brain to a sensor, a motor connection, or some other form of functional output. Under normal operating conditions, the organic brain inside a cybernetic body would interact with the body's non-autonomous systems in much the same way that the brain inside a human body controls and receives input from the body's sensory organs, muscles, and nerves.

From the viewpoint of the "person" who continued to possess and control the organic brain, the brain would perform just as it had inside the organic body: the optic nerves would carry input from the visual sensors ("eyes"); the olfactory nerves would carry information received and analyzed through the chemical sampler in the "head"; the motor nerves would receive and transmit impulses from and to the new, improved body's electromechanical extremities. . . .

"The first sensations you will perceive during the reconnection will be related to the operation of the major muscle groups in the extremities, specifically the quadriceps and the deltoids." The anonymous man's words came back to mind almost simultaneously with the next new impression that came into Cris's brain:

I HAVE SHOULDERS. I HAVE LEGS.

Cris Holman's new body still could not move, but his brain knew the body was there.

THIS IS WHAT IT MUST BE LIKE TO BE PARALYZED. IF MY BRAIN WORKS AND MY MUSCLES WORK, WHY CAN'T I DO ANYTHING?

He was aware of his body, at least as far as it went, because the right nerves had been connected to the right circuits, but he wasn't being allowed to function on full power.

Resistors built into the interface circuitry insured that only an infinitesimal trickle of neural/electrical energy could get through from his brain to his muscles — just enough power for the technicians to be able to trace its path and determine that the circuit was complete and correct, but not enough to enable his brain to move his extremities of its own volition. When all of his motor nerves were properly connected, someone would throw a switch, and . . .

"As the process continues, you will become aware of the lower ends of your body's arms and legs. You will feel capable of gradually more and more sophisticated movements."

NOW I CAN BEND MY ELBOW. BUT . . . IT WON'T. NOW MY KNEES . . . NO. NOT TIME YET.

Some of the most difficult connections involved

the nerves that worked the lower arms and fingers, because the cybernetic body did not have fingers *per se*. The neural circuitry that formerly had operated his hand and finger muscles, which were capable of extremely fine and delicate movements, was being connected to other sorts of mechanisms that also required great precision to operate properly — the built-in weaponry that, to a large degree, was what set a Cyborg Commando apart from a biological human. Later, when he had relearned how to use the power of the nerves that operated his fingers and hands, Cris Holman would be able to fire a laser by raising his arm and pointing his knuckles; he would be able to send out a hemisphere of electromagnetic interference by simply turning his palms outward.

I AM . . . WHOLE. I HAVE A BODY AGAIN.

He was still unable to communicate with, or receive information from, whatever was around him. But now Cris Holman was an entity again, a . . . person. Never mind that he couldn't hear, couldn't see, couldn't smell, couldn't speak. He could think. And, suddenly, he could feel himself being *touched*.

I FEEL SOMETHING . . . PRESSURE ON MY SKIN. WEIGHT ON THE BOTTOMS OF MY FEET. I AM BALANCING . . . I AM STANDING!

At this point, more than thirty-two hours since the first incision had been made in the back of the neck of his organic body, Cris Holman was still, to all outward appearances, little more than an automaton — and an essentially helpless one at that. But inside, he felt as he always had — like a human being, like a man. He knew what he was, he had a very good general idea of what was happening to him, and now, for the first time since experiencing his moment of renewed awareness of himself (HOW LONG AGO WAS THAT?) he was anxious. Eager to see, to hear, to taste, to rejoin the human race.

"Once your motor nerves are connected and tested, work will begin on the reconnection of your sensory nerves to the proper input devices. Some candidates have found this process exhilarating, and others have been rather negatively upset by it. At any rate, you will doubtless have *some* extreme reaction to it. . . ."

Sssssssss . . .

WHAT? I *HEAR* SOMETHING!

The auditory circuits were the first of P-17's sensory mechanisms to be connected — this, on the advice of psychologists who had theorized long and hard about the effect on the human psyche of bringing someone back from the almost-dead. The regaining of sight first, they said, might be too much of a shock to the brain — too much new information to assimilate all at once, after going through a period where it had received no visual input whatsoever.

Reconnecting the olfactory circuits first, on the other hand, might induce panic, because man did not consider his sense of smell essential to survival. The mind might assume that since the really important senses, sight and hearing, weren't working, that something was wrong: How come all I can do is *smell*?

So, through a process of elimination that they made to appear much more complicated than it actually was, the psychologists decided that the best thing to do first was (as one technician had informally put it a couple of seconds ago) "turn on the ears."

The hissing sound that Cris Holman's brain picked up was nothing more than the sound of gently moving air making its way across his body's auditory receptors — the only sound that no one in the surgical chamber could prevent, and a sound that would have been imperceptible if P-17's hearing had been only as sensitive as a normal human's. No one in the room was within twenty feet of his body, and all of them were holding their breath. If he had heard the boom of a heartbeat or the roar of an exhalation at that moment, the effect on his brain would have been many times worse than being awakened from a deep sleep by the clash of cymbals right next to his ear.

Fortunately, the sensitivity of his hearing was adjustable (and later, he would learn how to do this for himself). As soon as the technicians monitoring his brain activity ascertained that his auditory circuits had been activated, they knew that they had registered the sound of a "breeze" that was too faint to be felt on the skin. This meant that P-17's auditory system was functioning properly, and the engineers quickly adjusted the level of sensitivity downward so that the people in the room could start breathing and moving around again.

"Welcome back, P-17."

THE VOICE OF . . . TRAYNOR? COULD IT BE? HARD TO TELL.

"In answer to what you're probably thinking — yes, this is Traynor. You'll be fine-tuned pretty soon, and we're going to be seeing a lot of each other."

SEEING . . . EYES. I NEED EYES!

"Everything we've finished with is working well. We're getting pretty good at this by now. But we're going to keep you immobile while we finish up, and then you're going to have a lot of learning to do in a very short time."

FINISH UP? I NEED EYES! I NEED TO SPEAK! I AM *NOT* FINISHED, AND NEITHER ARE YOU PEOPLE!

Two hours later, Cris Holman could see again. Or, at least, he knew he would be able to see — if they'd let him look at something. Traynor broke in to explain.

"Your visual sensors are hooked up now, as I'm sure you already know. In a few minutes we're going to raise the protective covers — your eyelids — just a sliver. You won't be able to see much at first except for the difference between light and dark, but don't worry. As you pass through the sensitivity and definition tests, we'll increase the openings. About five minutes later, you'll be able to visualize and record any image that passes directly in front of you. But you won't be able to see up, down, or to the sides until later, when we fully power up your motor circuits."

WHITE, SQUARE.
BLACK, ROUND.
WHITE, TRIANGULAR.
BLACK. GRAY. LIGHT GRAY. DARK GRAY. YELLOW. DARK GREEN. RED. ORANGE. YELLOW-ORANGE. . . .

The different colors and shapes flashed before his eyes so quickly that, at first, Cris Holman's brain didn't have an opportunity to exult over regaining the power of sight. As each color and shape registered on his perception and triggered his recall of its name, the technicians' monitors confirmed that all was well with his visual sensors and the circuits that connected them to his brain. Then the screen on which the colors and shapes had been projected was removed from his narrow field of vision, and Cris saw where he was.

A short person, gender and age indistinguishable because of the smock and mask that covered all but his (HER?) eyes, stood directly in front of him for a couple of seconds. Then the person's eyes looked away, the face seemed to change expression beneath the mask, and he (SHE?) moved briskly to the side, out of view.

WANTED TO BE THE FIRST PERSON I SAW, I SUPPOSE. DON'T KNOW WHAT DIFFERENCE THAT MAKES — HOW WOULD I EVER RECOGNIZE SOMEONE BENEATH ALL THAT PLASTICLOTH?

Cris was momentarily perplexed by what he saw next — or, rather, what he didn't see. There was practically nothing going on in front of him. He could see the floor (WHITE, FLAT, HORIZONTAL), the opposite wall (DITTO, BUT VERTICAL), and a couple of benches where people sat, staring at monitor screens and occasionally making marks or writing phrases on charts. Then he focused his hearing on sounds of activity coming from behind him, muffled as though he was hearing them through a window.

OF COURSE — THAT'S WHERE ALL THE WORK IS GOING ON. SURE WOULD BE NICE TO HAVE EYES IN THE BACK OF MY HEAD. . . .

An hour later, Cris Holman's brain could smell — and the first odor that he registered was no odor at all, only the antiseptic non-smell of the small, sterile world in which he was being reincarnated. Just as he was beginning to wonder why they weren't giving his new nose a chance to do its stuff, Traynor's voice — again — came through his ear-speaker to tell him what he wanted to know, which informed him and reassured him at the same time.

"We'll test your olfactory circuits and your sampler later, when we've moved you outside the controlled environment. If we contaminate this room with the odor of smelly chemicals and the taste of delicious flavors, the sanitation workers' union will have a fit."

Ninety minutes after that, Cris Holman's brain felt a low vibration emanating from what passed for his throat, just as he was in the middle of "saying" — for the hundredth or so time — what he was thinking at the moment:

I WISH THESE METER-READERS WOULD—

"—get this tin suit zipped up so I can start moving around!"

And is it any wonder, thought Traynor as he chuckled silently, why we always save the vocal circuits for last?

It considered the resistance significant not because It feared for the outcome of the battle, but because anything less than the utter annihilation of the human race and its technology was unacceptable. Relishing the prospect, It began thinking about ways to make Its minions even more gruesome and deadly. . . .

19

February 4-6, 2035

I'M GLAD THEY CAN'T SEE ME BLUSH . . .

"Don't feel bad," said Traynor in his ear. "It happens to almost everyone."

. . . OR CAN THEY?

"In fact, we have a motto around here: You have to fall before you can crawl."

Ten seconds after Cyborg Commando P-17 was placed on full internal power for the first time, Cris Holman's brain told P-17's right leg to take one giant step forward. In the instant after his right foot left the ground, his right knee was suddenly level with his waist. He teetered on his left foot, felt his torso bend and dip to the left in an attempt to compensate, and in less time than it takes to describe it he found himself face down, sprawled out on the floor of the training room. He froze, not

daring to move another mechanical muscle — AM I
HOOKED UP RIGHT? — until he found out what was
going on.

"What happened?"

"In simple terms," said Traynor, "you tried too
hard. You were concentrating on taking a step,
breaking down the motion into all of its component
movements. At first, for some reason we haven't
figured out yet, that's how the conscious mind
thinks it has to operate in order to work the cybernetic body. The sooner you start perceiving yourself as a whole, instead of as the sum of a bunch
of parts, the sooner you'll get over your clumsiness
— and the less damage you'll do to the things you
fall over and bump into."

Cris almost hated to admit it, but the man was
right. YEAH, I DO REMEMBER THINKING, 'THE FIRST THING
I HAVE TO DO IS GET MY FOOT UP OFF THE GROUND.' THEN
. . . SPLAT!

"So what do I do now? Lay here and wait for the
garbage pickup?"

"Just relax, give yourself a few minutes. Try a
little bit of meditation. Then, without thinking about
it *consciously*, tell yourself to get up."

"How am I supposed to tell myself to do something without thinking about doing it?"

"You used to do it all the time, and you can do it
again. Just give it a try. The worst you can do is
put another dent in the floor."

So, Cris tried not to try . . . and it worked! After

taking a couple of minutes to calm down, he simply said to himself, BETTER GET UP NOW. His elbows and knees bent in tandem — slowly, a little jerkily, but together. His hands pushed down against the floor, causing his torso to move in the opposite direction, and (without thinking about it!) he was on his hands and knees.

"Very good!" said Traynor, raising his voice to a level of volume and enthusiasm Cris had not heard him use before. "Now, when you're ready, up the rest of the way. . . ."

Standing up was harder than getting to all fours. He was afraid to use too much oomph and topple himself over backward, so he pushed off with his arms half-heartedly the first time and dropped forward again, catching himself on his elbows just before his face would have hit the floor for a second time. He took the cybernetic equivalent of a couple of deep breaths, forced himself to not think about what he was trying to do (it was already getting easier!), and just let it happen.

He pushed off with his hands and simultaneously allowed his torso to start moving into an orientation that would put it perpendicular to the floor. As he thought about STANDING UP, without worrying about all of the parts of his body that had to cooperate to make that happen, he straightened into a semi-squat. After holding that position for a half-second to make sure he was stable — just as a human being might do — he allowed his legs to unbend, and just like that he was on his feet.

"What an accomplishment," Cris said, feeling proud of himself and, at the same time, a little embarrassed because he was proud of such a trivial success — something a two-year-old child could have done faster and better.

"No mean feat," said Traynor, "and you picked it up pretty quickly. But you have a lot more to learn, so don't get a swelled head."

"No danger of that, Doc. From what they tell me, one size fits all."

*   *   *

For the next three days, Cris Holman's brain and P-17's body went through a program of education and fine tuning that brought the two elements closer and closer into synchronization with each other. Cris's sphere of knowledge, his degree of familiarity with his new form, grew geometrically. Every time he learned how to do one more specific thing, it seemed, that triumph would open doors to a dozen new accomplishments. And each of those passages, when it was investigated, would lead to ten or twelve or twenty others. . . .

Through it all, Traynor was his only constant companion. The man encouraged, prodded, chided, scolded. He was in charge of telling Cris *what* to do, but conveniently (or so it seemed to Cris) never could or would tell him *how*.

"You think this is easy?" Cris snapped after trying and failing for the third time to open an electronic combination lock. "I could have done this on the first try with a set of real fingers, instead of these lousy extruded-metal excuses for digits. And all you do is sit there and sigh. Give it a try, smart guy!" he said, moving back away from the locked door panel and gesturing toward the lock with a stiff flourish.

"As a matter of fact," Traynor shot back, "I could do it with 'lousy metal fingers,' because I happen to know the access code. But that's not the point. *You* have to do it — and once you do, your inboard computer will record exactly what sequence of movements you need to duplicate in order to do it over and over again."

The purpose of the post-operation training was twofold. Part of Cris's time was spent learning how to cause his organic brain to operate as an integral part of his cybernetic body — a process that involved, as did standing up, learning how to do things without thinking about how they were done. The other part was, in a very literal sense, a programming exercise.

The process went something like this: When Cris's organic brain called upon P-17's body to perform some small-scale chore that required precision, deftness, or some form of dexterity, and if that task was something that could be successfully re-performed at any time by exactly duplicating a series of movements, that data would be stored in the pseudomemory of P-17's inboard computer.

Then, when Cris's brain recognized a recurrence of the same situation, control for the performance of the task would automatically be passed to the computer, which would then direct the proper extremities to do the right things at the right times. This did not constitute a pre-empting of the organic brain, but rather a reinforcement of it. Cris's brain might also remember how to do the task at hand, but the human brain is not one hundred percent consistent, not reliable when it comes to recalling how to do something the same way every time it is attempted.

"I like that," Cris had said to himself during training when he was told about the way his brain would be computer-enhanced. "It's a real crunch to have to look up how to recalibrate my lasercorder every time the power company has a slumpdown." As it turned out, he had the right idea, but his sense of how the capability would be used was far removed from what actually happened.

Well . . . perhaps not that far removed. At least the principle was the same. But now he was educating himself to perform tasks more important than recalibrating a lasercorder. Tasks that, mundane as they seemed, might someday mean the difference between life and death — or, as the techs liked to put it in their less humane moments, power-on and power-off.

Cris did not need to be told that any single aspect of what he was doing, what he was learning, could turn out to be the thing that kept him in a power-on condition. Despite his frequent vocal resistance and his occasional, unvoiced frustration and rebellion, he was dedicated. Beyond that, he was committed.

In moments of whimsy, Cris likened his situation to that of being brought back in the body of . . . pick an animal, any animal. The brain that had once operated a human body (and, fate willing, would operate one — the same one — again) was for the immediate future faced with the depressing yet challenging prospect of learning how to make a nonhuman body function to the best of its (the brain's and the body's) ability.

"If I were a dog," Cris thought, "I'd have to learn how to eat — how to *enjoy* eating — without using my hands. Could that be any worse than what I'm trying to learn right now?"

The answer he arrived at was "no." Different, maybe, but not worse. At least, in this incarnation, he had a body that his brain could relate to. A head resting firmly yet fluidly on a neck, which was connected to a torso; a head that seemed to have all the right parts (externally) in all the right places. Arms and legs, hands and feet, fingers and toes — an entire body covered with super-tough yet super-flexible skin of a uniform pale brown color.

Even after specially sculpted armor plating was

fastened around his torso and legs, P-17's cybernetic body was very humanlike in most of the outwardly visible ways. His head and arms were left unarmored so that he looked not like a robot but like a man. It was impressed upon Cris during testing that, because cybernetic bodies looked so much like human ones, every Cyborg Commando would be seen by all of mankind as a heroic figure, capable of achievements that humans could never realize — such as blasting the monstrous invaders out of existence.

I DON'T FEEL MUCH LIKE A HERO RIGHT NOW. Frustration was giving way to self-doubt as Cris continued to struggle with the dials of the lock. I CAN'T EVEN OPEN THIS DAMN DOOR. . . .

He went through all the same steps he had taken three times before, perceiving no reason to change what he was doing. Then he felt it — an ever-so-slight, ever-so-brief trace of friction as he slowly pushed a lever along a slot marked with gradations. He backed up over the same spot and felt it again.

Traynor noticed the backtracking movement instantly and held his breath. The thumb and finger of P-17's right hand nudged the lever a half-millimeter back in the original direction, then left the small protrusion in place and reached for a dial positioned just beneath it. The dial gave off a small electrical charge when it was in position, a trickle of voltage that a human fingertip could not have felt, but which P-17's fingertip, once it was properly positioned on the lever, detected as readily as if the charge had been a hundred times stronger.

A careful quarter-turn, and abruptly the charge was there, trickling into his finger and through his body. The lever had been the critical factor; Cris's ability to feel that tiny bit of current had enabled him to position the lever so that it controlled the circuit that turned on the power running through the dial. Were all the pieces of the puzzle finally in place? Only one way to find out. . . .

With his right hand still holding the dial on the zero point, Cris reached up with his left, pushed the latch-button . . . and the door sprang open into an adjoining room.

"Presto!" Cris shouted. "I knew I had it in me!"

"You didn't before," said Traynor. "But you do now."

* * *

The last phase of Cris's indoctrination was education in the use of his body's built-in weaponry and defense systems — or, as a handmade sign on the wall of the training chamber put it, "Monster Mashing 101."

Before the operation, Cris had been given a thorough briefing on what his new body could do in the areas of attack and defense. The people who ran the program knew that a Cyborg Commando's weaponry was one of its biggest drawing cards, one of the aspects that most attracted prospective candidates, so they went into quite a bit of detail about a CC's armament and defense capabilities in the early stages of training. Being able to see beyond the normal visible spectrum was nice; being able to hear an insect bump into a pane of glass from twenty-five feet away could be useful at times; but no one would have wanted to be turned into a cybernetic soldier if the deal didn't include ways to blast things to smithereens and ways to keep from being blasted.

"Hold it! I think . . . I think something's going wrong, Traynor!"

Cris hadn't felt a thing when a technician peeled back a small slice of pseudoskin and opened up a panel in the lower rear of his torso, except for a pleasant sensation that felt as though someone was scratching his back. But now, all of a sudden, a soft but strange feeling of warmth was spreading through his forearms and his lower legs.

"Relax," said Traynor.

"Am I on overload, or what?"

"Quite the opposite. Until now, you've been on underload, in a manner of speaking — your weapons systems haven't been charged. The warmth you feel is an indication that you are now ready to aim and fire — and it's a feeling you'd better learn to enjoy. If it ever goes away while you're in the field, that means you're defenseless."

"Traynor, you can be *so* encouraging."

"Just want you to know what you're up against."

"Right now all I'm up against is you. Are you gonna tell me how to use all these gadgets, or do I just start trying 'em out?"

Using his "military features," as Traynor called them, was easy, fun, and a little scary for Cris all at the same time.

Easy, because by now his brain was very good at getting his new body to do what he wanted it to — even though this body had some decidedly non-human attributes. For instance, he didn't have to actually learn how to project a laser beam out of his knuckles; all he had to do was form his fingers into a partial fist, point his knuckles at the target, and think FIRE. Best of all, he couldn't blow up anything valuable or important (such as a human being) by accident; the sensors monitored by his inboard computer took care of that. If he made a fist in the direction of something that was not an enemy or should not (according to the computer) be destroyed, the weapon would simply not fire.

Fun, because despite its life-or-death undertones, this was what being a Cyborg Commando was all about. It was fun to think of yourself as invincible (although, of course, that wasn't literally true), able to both cause and resist destruction, and to do both by means of an array of weapons and defense systems that were the most advanced and most powerful that man had devised for use on this scale. It would be no fun to use these awesome, terrible powers on a man or any other creature native to Earth — but to be able to wade into a group of aliens and wade back out leaving them in a broken, lifeless pile . . . well, that prospect gave new meaning to the word "exhilaration."

Scary — just a little — for the same reasons that made it fun. When he saw just what his weaponry was capable of, through personal experimentation in the training chamber and the viewing of videotapes, Cris could not help but feel the cybernetic equivalent of a shiver. "What happens if something goes wrong?" he asked Traynor. "What if something I don't want to hit gets in the way?"

"The answers to those questions should be patently obvious," the man responded. "I think what you really want to know is how to keep such a thing from happening — and that I can't tell you. Once you're outside this sanitized, high-tech womb, you'll have to make sure that doesn't happen, or deal with it if it does."

"That was a lousy answer."

"It's the only one I've got."

20

February 6, 2035

Nora sat in the audience section of the training room with the few members of the base personnel who were able to spare a few minutes to watch. Before the invasion of the bug-creatures the twenty-foot-square, boxed-in section was continually full of observers, curious about the day-to-day progress of the super-soldiers they were helping to create. But now there were more urgent matters at hand and when they had any free time, most of the overworked employees stationed at the Manitowoc base spent it getting some well-deserved rest.

Nora knew all of the spectators there today by name except for one — a young man, sitting next to her at the moment, whom she had seen in this room on each of the last three days. She was more than a little curious about him. But right now she was more interested in watching her son struggle to manipulate an electronic combination lock. Cris, or P-17 as he was now known, was unable to make his new fingers properly manipulate the device and, after three tries, was getting frustrated. And he was getting no assistance from Traynor.

Nora knew that Traynor was acting in her son's best interest, but she couldn't help feeling a pang of motherly sympathy for Cris. It was agonizing to watch him suffer like this, and even more painful to have to sit by and do nothing. She couldn't even offer him any words of comfort.

Nora felt no small amount of relief when, suddenly, mercifully, Cris mastered the art of breaking the electronic code.

"Presto!" Cris shouted. "I knew I had it in me!"

Nora felt a surge of pride when Traynor answered, "You didn't before. But you do now."

"Way to go!" the young man next to Nora whistled softly.

"Not bad for a novice, huh, pal?" P-17's metallic voice answered back from more than fifty feet away.

"How did he hear me?" the young man asked aloud, not really expecting an answer.

"His new 'ears' are quite a bit sharper than yours and mine," Nora said to him. "He could hear us whispering from a hundred yards away if he wanted to."

"Wow!" he said wistfully. Then he introduced

himself. "Thanks for the input. My name's Tony Minelli, and I volunteered for this program. But, alas, they didn't think this wimpy body of mine would keep well on ice."

"Hello, Tony. I'm Nora Whitaker. I'm—"

"Nora Whitaker! I know that name!" Tony interrupted her. "You practically invented the Cyborg Commando! I heard all about you in the briefing sessions after I volunteered."

Nora smiled. "I didn't 'practically invent' the CC, or even the concept. But I have had a lot to do with making the concept a reality."

"Hey, good enough. It's a pleasure to meet you!" Tony said, reaching out and offering his hand.

Nora took it and shook it courteously. Then she asked, "So what are you doing here if you were turned down for the program, Tony?"

"I got lucky," he said. "They gave me a job recording data during physical examinations. Even though I'd still rather be a CC, I can't complain — it's interesting work, and it keeps me down here away from those gruesome creatures. Besides, Cris — I mean P-17 — and I have become almost like brothers in the last few weeks. I haven't seen much of him lately, but I've been keeping close track of how he's doing."

"How did you meet?" Nora asked, almost afraid to hope she was about to get some information about her son's prior existence.

"We both attended the university at Whitewater, although we never spoke until after those . . . things . . . invaded. I met Cris when he came to Whitewater on the first night with his little sister. They were looking for Cris's girlfriend, but they never found her. I found out later that Cris lived in Delavan, and the creatures had killed both of his parents. Anyway, I was a volunteer on guard duty and stopped Cris as he came into . . ."

Tony continued, but Nora had stopped listening. So Marc was dead. . . . She was surprised at the pang of sadness that news caused her to feel. But her sorrow quickly turned to surprise and frustration as she realized that Cris had been living — perhaps for the last several years — within driving distance of where she was working!

". . . So, when we saw the bus that Sara had been riding in overturned in the snow, and it was obvious that there were no survivors—"

"Excuse me," Nora said, standing up suddenly. "I'm not feeling very well." And with that she hurriedly left the room.

Gee, I hope she's okay, Tony thought, and then turned his attention back to P-17, whose jubilation over his newfound skill had toned down considerably. Tony chuckled. P-17 was definitely not enjoying himself. Traynor was now insisting that he practice making delicate movements with his feet against a series of pressure plates. The first few times he tried, Cris pressed too hard, and each of these small failures was punctuated by a word of disgust.

"Maybe being rejected for this program wasn't such a bad thing after all," Tony mused softly.

"I heard that, Minelli." P-17's metallic voice boomed from across the room, and Tony jumped.

* * *

Nora angrily pulled her bottom desk drawer open and removed a key ring. She walked across the room and unlocked the file cabinet. With frantic haste she pulled open the bottom drawer and rifled through it until she found what she was looking for buried beneath a stack of papers. She had unscrewed the cap and was raising the bottle to her lips when a voice interrupted her.

"You don't really want to do that."

Nora whirled around to face C-12. "John! What right have you to walk in here unannounced? This is my office, and—"

"Come on, Nora, don't say anything you don't really mean," John said in a soothing voice. Nora noticed the absence of his metallic monotone and temporarily forgot everything else.

"John! You sound . . . normal! I wasn't aware that you were scheduled for a voice adjustment, or that it was even possible to perform such a procedure on any of the older cyborgs—"

"First of all," C-12 said as he reached out and

took the bottle from Nora's hand, "you weren't 'aware' because I wanted it to be a surprise, and I asked that the information be kept from you."

"But how—"

"It wasn't easy! I had to assure a few people that you wouldn't raise hell when you found out you had been kept in the dark. So don't make a liar out of me, okay?"

"I won't," Nora smiled. "It's a nice surprise."

"And as far as us 'older cyborgs' go, this older cyborg is only three years old, and the body that goes with its brain is all of twenty-four. Since when have those two ages been considered 'old'?" C-12 asked with all the indignation he could manage, purposely taking every opportunity to exercise his new voice.

"Oh, John, it's wonderful to hear you sounding like . . . yourself. I can't tell you how often I've longed to hear that voice again!" Nora was genuinely moved, and suddenly the anger and frustration she had felt minutes earlier gave way to a flood of tears.

John listened sympathetically as she tearfully told him about how she had learned of Marc Holman's death and of the discovery that, maybe for years, she had been working within mere miles of her son and didn't even know it. All the sadness, bitterness, and anger that had been stored inside for so long came out with such force that when it was over, Nora was exhausted. John talked her into lying down on the couch in her office and promised to sit with her until she fell asleep.

"John, what will happen to my son?" Nora asked.

"He'll be fine. Not only fine, he'll be a hero some day. After all, he'll have one hell of a partner when he goes into combat."

"You *know* who he's teamed up with?" Nora started to sit up.

"Yep," John answered, a wide grin spread across his face. "Another piece of information you haven't been told yet."

"Well, tell me now. Which of the new recruits did they pair him with? P-10? P-13?"

"Nope. You weren't listening. I *said* he got the best."

"But those two *are* the best!" Nora argued.

"Not by a long shot, lady. You're *looking* at the best. And don't you forget it!"

John enjoyed the feeling as C-12's visual sensors saw the expression change on Nora's face. "You!? But how—" she sputtered.

"Clout, my dear, clout. Something we 'older models' have a lot of these days."

"Oh John, take care of him, please. And take care of yourself. I don't think I could bear losing either of you."

"You just rest. Nothing's going to happen to me or Cris. I give you my personal guarantee."

John stayed until Nora's steady, deep breathing

assured him she was asleep. Then he stood, picked up the bottle of scotch he had taken from her earlier, walked into the bathroom, and dumped the liquor down the drain. He dropped the bottle in a waste container, flipped the switch, and watched as it was ground to bits.

John walked over to the couch where Nora lay sleeping. "I love you," he said very softly. Then he left her alone.

21

February 7, 2035

Cris Holman had a body that didn't get tired or sick. P-17 would never feel physical fatigue, or anything resembling it, as long as its power cells were kept sufficiently charged. But Cris's brain still needed to sleep . . . to dream.

To keep his brain psychologically and physically healthy, Cris had to allow it to rest for an average of between four and six hours out of every twenty-four — an aspect that Traynor had once described to Cris, in a moment of unappreciated levity, as "an unavoidable design flaw."

Flaw or not, the technicians had made good use of the obligatory sleep periods during Cris's indoctrination, spending the hours performing minor maintenance and fine tuning on P-17's circuitry and mechanisms — purposeful tinkering that would have wasted time if it had been performed while Cris's brain was awake, since he would have been able to do nothing else in the meantime.

Each time he had come out of sleep, Cris had been pleasantly surprised to find out that some particular aspects of P-17's body worked a little better than they had before. At first, for instance, it had been difficult for him to distinguish between the smell of burning rubber and the odor of burning plastic. He didn't see why it mattered, but Traynor told him that "You never know when a little difference will turn out to be a big one. We'll have it fixed, and then you won't have to worry." Sure enough, after his next sleep period, he performed perfectly on a second olfactory examination.

Before he entered the sleep period he was now in, Cris had been told that when he woke, he would be put through final, brief preparations for P-17's first mission. Cris pressed Traynor for details, but the man either could not or would not give him any.

As he slid into sleep, Cris forced himself to concentrate on what tomorrow would bring. He tried to imagine himself leaping through a door into the outside world, taking one look around, and immediately starting to mutilate or incinerate one miserable bug-monster after another. . . .

"Hey, headquarters. This is Cris."

"Repeat and clarify. 'Kriss' is not a standard designation."

"Bullshit. It was standard when I was born."

"Frequency analysis complete. We have identified the communicating unit as P-17."

"Aw, call me Pee, and I'll call you Head."

"Why have you initiated radio contact, P-17?"

"Just thought you . . . humans . . . would like to know I'm all finished up out here and I'm coming back in. Have a nice, cold glass of liquid graphite lubricant ready for me."

"It is not necessary for you to ingest liquid graphite lubricant."

"You know what I mean. . . . No, I suppose you don't."

"P-17, Access Bay C will be prepared for your use. Proceed along the most direct route possible. Our monitors indicate your power supply has dropped to recharge level. All motive and weapons systems remain fully operational, but response time of inboard computer is slightly slower than normal. Exercise caution."

"I always exercise caution. My caution is in great shape."

A blur of motion, a rat-a-tat of shapes and sounds passed across Cris's vision as he backtracked toward headquarters. He saw smoking, moldering heaps of alien flesh — the despicable creatures he had incinerated on his way out. Their decomposing bodies were at the same time horrible and wonderful to behold. Cris felt triumphant, exultant, and very, very sure of himself.

"Hey, Pee. Head here. Get it into gear, willya? We just picked up a flock of bugs heading for the same place you're goin'."

"Huh? What? Who is this really?"

"Quit playin' dumb and motivate if you wanna have a home to come back to by the time you get here."

"Not again! Those spit-sucking bugs aren't going to ruin this home like they did my last one. If I can't beat them to the door, I'll blast them away from it!"

"Nice talk, Pee. But talk is cheap. Whaddya got to back it up with?"

"This!" Cris thrust out his right fist, and a sparkling, searing beam of concentrated light shot out. He swung his hand back and forth in an arc in front of his body, cutting a thumb-thick incision into and through everything the beam touched. At the same time, he broke into a sprint and made a beeline for Access Bay C, choosing to ignore the inboard computer's emotionless message about how he was dangerously close to a power-off condition.

He destroyed without discrimination as he ran, a one-man (one-thing? half-man?) laser-beam buzz-saw. Waves of pure emotion washed over him in rapid succession — panic, anger, pleasure, panic, anger, . . .

. . . pleasure! Now the entryway was in sight, and — even better news! — the only thing that stood between him and safety was a lone alien, in a form that looked something like a scorpion, positioned defiantly and foolishly in front of the doorway. Cris felt his legs starting to give out, his laser starting to weaken, but he knew he had enough power left to fry this stupid bug!

He swung his arm around to face the alien and heard the characteristic crackle-sizzle of its body being chopped and cooked at the same time. He played the beam back and forth across the ugly body three or four times, cutting it into smaller and smaller chunks. Finally, the pieces collapsed, and the ten-foot-tall buglike thing was reduced to a two-foot-high pile of amorphous parts.

As the creature collapsed, P-17's internal power system drew the last feeble impulse from its all-but-dead batteries. Cris's legs stopped moving, his laser went out as though he had turned it off, and the only part of his body that still worked was his visual circuitry.

As P-17 stood paralyzed, he saw that something else now stood between him and the door. There, leaning against the door, clutching his charred torso and wearing a look of shocked, pitiful bewilderment, was the already dead body of Marc Holman. . . .

"No! No! Not again!"

Cris was screaming when he woke up — screaming in *his* voice!

He noticed the difference instantly, and in the

next second of realization he had already started to push the memory of his awful dream back into his mind, to be replaced in the forefront by wonderment and puzzlement over the way he sounded.

"Relax." It was the familiar, and this time soothing, voice of Traynor.

"Where? . . . What? . . . How . . . ?" Just as he had always been, Cris was slow to wake up. As his brain tried to form the questions he wanted answers to, the nightmare faded rapidly into the background. He still would be able to recall it in vivid detail for days, but he would remember it as a dream, not as the horrible reality it had first seemed to be. And he would try not to forget the lesson that his subconscious mind had taught him.

In his semi-muddled state, Cris reached out and pressed the palm of his right hand against his left forearm. It felt like flesh, but it wasn't flesh. His voice sounded the way it had before the operation, but he was most definitely still encased in an artificial body. "Traynor . . . what's wrong? Am I changing back? I don't sound like I should."

"On the contrary," said Traynor. "You sound exactly like you should. While you were asleep, we installed an electronic larynx tailored to your voice pattern — one of our latest improvements. You're still equipped with the voice modulators you had been using for verbal communication, but that system is wired in as a backup now."

Cris took a couple of minutes to put his new

voicebox through its paces. He recited the alphabet deliberately, enjoying the sound of his own voice all the way through. When he said the letter B, it felt as though he was closing and opening his lips, even though his artificial face had no such parts. On the letter L, he felt his nonexistent tongue press against his nonexistent upper palate. When he got to P, he said the letter twice, and noticed each time that he tended to expel a bit too much air as he parted his lips — the same insignificant but noticeable (to therapists, anyway) quirk in his speech pattern that he had had all his life.

"I like it . . . I think," he said to Traynor after drawing out the letter Z and tacking on a few nonsensical sound effects for good measure. "It is a little eerie, though, hearing my own voice come out of something that isn't me."

"Would you like us to take it back and make you sound like some child's toy robot?"

"I didn't say *that*. It's just—"

"You've got to stop thinking of yourself as *not* yourself. All the parts that make you who you are still reside inside the body you happen to be occupying. These arms and legs are not *you*, but they are *your* arms and legs — and, if you'd just look at it that way, the same could be said for the arms and legs of your human body."

"I know what you're getting at," said Cris. "But you're not inside one of these contraptions. It's just kind of hard to . . . relate to, that's all," he finished, groping for a way to finish the sentence and feeling unsatisfied with the words he had chosen.

Yes, Traynor thought, you're right. I can't relate to it, either. But I don't have to . . . and I'm sorry you do.

* * *

Following Traynor, and consciously shortening the length of his stride to avoid overrunning the man, Cris passed through a sliding door into a part of the base he had not seen before. The small sign next to the doorway said it all: "Mission Briefing."

This is it! Cris thought, almost bringing his right foot down on Traynor's right heel as he forgot himself for a moment. This is what I came for!

Minutes later, Cris found himself thinking that it was a good thing he had a face that didn't mirror his emotions. He felt his facial muscles work — his brow furrowed, his nose wrinkled, and in a moment of self-indulgence, his lower lip moved outward ever so slightly. But, as he knew, all of that activity was taking place only in his brain. P-17's face, as it always had and always would, remained impassive and expressionless.

"I suppose this doesn't sound all that exciting," said Traynor — how did he know? — "but if you try to be objective about it, you'll see why we can't just send you out on a combat mission right away."

As he spoke, Cris abandoned any attempt at

concealing his feelings. "Well," he said in his best petulant tone, "I'm not looking at things very objectively right now, and I especially don't understand why I have to go through even more testing."

"This mission is not a test," said Traynor with a slight edge in his voice. "Granted, operating well in laboratory conditions is not the same as operating well in the field. We can't possibly anticipate, much less simulate, everything that might happen to you outside this environment, so we will be monitoring and recording your performance. But that information will only be useful to us, and to you, if and when you make it back."

Traynor paused for a beat, took a step toward his student, and shot forth a glare that conveyed concern more than anger. "Once you get out there, you're going to be on your own — on your own for the first time in this . . . in your life."

That was the first time Cris could remember the man correcting himself, the first time he had said something . . . he wasn't supposed to say? No matter what the reason, Traynor's misstatement — and especially the way he rephrased the sentence — was all it took for Cris to come around. He enjoyed it and resented it at the same time, but there was no way to ignore the fact: This man reminded Cris very much of his father. And he had always respected what his father said to him, even when he didn't understand it or agree with it.

"Okay, doc," he said, injecting a smile into his

voice to make up for the one he couldn't put on his face. "I get the picture."

"All right, P-17," said Traynor, moving abruptly back into official mode. "These are your mission parameters:

"You will leave this complex for a period of time not to exceed one hundred fifty minutes. During the time you are in the field, you are not to take any overt offensive action that is not essential to your survival. In other words, no target practice."

"But—"

"You will not move to engage any hostile or potentially hostile presence that you encounter or detect. In other words, no bug-swatting unless you get cornered. And don't get cornered."

"Aw, come on, Traynor—"

"You will at no time move farther than two and one-half miles away from the access bay you leave. You will at no time enter a structure or attempt to enter and operate any form of conveyance. You will—"

"What *can* I do?"

Traynor ignored the question. "You will at no time approach or accost any human being unless that person first attempts to communicate with you, and you will not present a threatening posture to any human being who speaks to you or otherwise acknowledges your presence. You will not subject your body to any form of stress or potential trauma that in your judgment, and the subsequent judgment of the monitoring technicians in this complex, is beyond the scope of what your body has been subjected to during your training and indoctrination."

"How do I know what *their* judgment will be?"

"That's all, P-17."

"That's it? What am I supposed to *do*?"

"Go out, move around, don't get in trouble, and get back. Needless to say, items three and four are the most important ones on the agenda."

"You make me feel like a kid who's taking the family car out for the first time." As soon as he said that, Cris wished he hadn't, because he knew, as Traynor immediately pointed out . . .

"In a very real way, that's pretty close to what you're doing. Go out with that attitude — sincerely — and you'll do all right." Traynor got that earnest, concerned look on his face again, and Cris knew the man wasn't in the mood for any more argument or banter.

"P-17 will do its . . . his best," Cris said.

Traynor looked visibly moved. Cris wondered what he might have done to bring this about, and then it came to him. Without thinking about it, he had referred to himself as—

"I know you will . . . Cris."

P-17 showed no emotion whatsoever. Inside, Cris Holman cried.

22

February 8, 2035

"Pee seventeen."

The light over the door in front of Cris went from white to green as the voice-actuated sensors in the lock reacted positively, opening the alarm and locking circuits and thereby allowing the door to be pushed open. Cris pushed the instep of his left foot lightly against a protrusion, and the six-inch-thick steel panel, meticulously counterbalanced, slid open slowly and smoothly. In the instant after he took his second step to get through the doorway, the panel slammed shut, propelled back to the closed position by super-strong electromagnets built into the grooved tracks.

The twenty-foot-diameter access tunnel was solid steel-reinforced concrete, and solid black. It didn't need to be illuminated, and Cris didn't need light in order to see. All he had to do was walk up the gradual incline, using low-intensity sound waves to keep himself moving in a straight line. If he started to get feedback, indicating he was closer to one side of the tunnel than the other (which did happen a few times), he simply shifted his next step slightly in the proper direction so that his path remained parallel to both walls.

In about two minutes he had traveled the length of the quarter-mile tunnel, strolling along at about twice normal human walking speed. His sonic emissions told Cris that the ceiling ahead of him was becoming lower, tapering to a point where, about forty feet beyond, it intersected with the still-inclined floor. This was his cue to stop and again say the name he had not yet, and probably never would, become accustomed to.

"Pee seventeen, about to bump my head."

Nothing happened.

"Peee . . . sev . . . en . . . teen." He said it slowly and carefully, like someone teaching another person a foreign language.

The ceiling in front of him shuddered slightly, dropped down about a foot, and then began to come apart into four sections, each of which was drawn along a perpendicular path into the top edge of the wall it was adjacent to. He kept looking straight ahead, tilted his head slightly upward, and P-17's eyes got their first look at the outside world.

When the ceiling had parted enough to allow him to walk through the opening, he did just that —

and as soon as he brought his trailing foot up out of the tunnel, the ceiling (which was now the ground, in relation to Cris's position) closed up in the space of about a second and a half.

When he turned around to look at the place he had just come through, all he could see with normal vision were four rectangular patches of asphalt, outwardly identical to the other patches on either side that made up a normal-looking roadway. "Boy," Cris mumbled, "they sure know how to make a guy feel wanted."

He was standing on an unspectacular stretch of pavement, at this spot inclined slightly in the opposite direction of the tunnel's slope, that ran south toward a small shopping center. From the looks of it, the road had been used as a way for delivery vehicles to get to and from the stores. In bygone days, it was also a route that supply trucks and personnel carriers took to get to the tunnel that would carry them into the underground research complex.

Now, however, the residents of the complex were not being served by the outside world. (The members of the military had more urgent demands on their time.) They were subsisting, and could get along for at least another year, on the equipment and supplies that had been stored within and beneath the complex — necessities that had been stockpiled to guard against a catastrophe perpetrated by man upon man, but were just as life-saving in this time of tragedy caused by something other than man.

Cris took a look around and didn't see anything that seemed out of the ordinary. "The only thing unpleasant in this area is the cold!" he said.

That made him think — and, by ordering it to occur, Cris raised his subsurface and pseudoskin temperature to compensate for the chilly air. If he had failed to do so consciously, his internal computer would have made the temperature adjustment on its own in another two or three minutes, before his skin began to stiffen and lose some of its elasticity.

One effect of the temperature adjustment became immediately apparent: As Cris walked along the snow-covered roadway, he left large, oval-shaped bare spots where his feet melted the ice and snow they touched, and some of the ice and snow around it, in much the same way that a hot knife will make a hole in a block of ice much larger around than the knife blade itself. The difference in this case was that the knife blade would eventually, and probably quickly, cool off, but Cris's body would maintain its surface temperature of about 66 degrees Centigrade until he specified differently, or until his internal computer detected a reason why it should override his organic brain and order a change.

Cris made his way north to the nearest two-lane street, then walked west, down the center of the pavement, until he came to an intersection with another thoroughfare. So far the only signs of life he had seen were the footprints of people and occasional tracks left by dogs and cats in the snow, none of the routes having any organization or definite direction to them. The street was devoid of any sign that it had been used for vehicular traffic recently, at least not since the last snow had fallen.

"What do I do?" Cris said to himself. "There's nothing to kill and nobody to protect." Then he remembered that his orders didn't permit him to do any killing (and probably not any protecting either), but that realization didn't do much to counteract his disappointment and mild irritation. He stopped in the dead center of the intersection, as if daring someone or something to run him over, or at least notice him. "So what *am* I supposed to do? Walk for a while, turn around, and—"

Then he heard it. A soft crunch. Another, and another, and another. . . . Something was moving through the snow, away from him — running! — down the street and off to his right, about half a block from where he stood.

So, Cris ran too. From a standing start, he erupted in two strides to a speed of roughly thirty miles per hour. Almost before he realized it, he had traveled several hundred feet — and overshot the place where he should have turned off the street. With one emphatic stomp of his right foot, he stopped his forward momentum, plowing a six-foot-long hot scar in the snow in the process. He turned around and set off at a slow trot — a mere fifteen miles per hour — for a few paces until he pulled up even with an open space between two buildings.

As he turned to his left, Cris saw a body topped by unkempt but fairly short hair, clothed in a worn but still usable winter jacket, a pair of tight, probably insulated pants, and a pair of shin-high, too-large plastirubber boots . . . a person, out in the open!

The two seconds that he hesitated probably made the difference between Cris's being able to intercept the man and his inability to do so. As soon as he got over his initial amazement at seeing another living thing, Cris took off into the fifteen-foot-wide strip of open space at a speed almost equal to that of his earlier sprint. He shouted "Hey!" in a voice so loud that it scared him (but not enough to make him break his stride), and the object of his communication gave a brief glance over his shoulder.

At the same instant, Cris raised a hand in greeting — which, if anything, made the man ahead of him move even faster, half-leaping through the snow as fast as his ill-equipped feet would carry him, staying close to the building on his right even though the going was tougher where the snow had drifted up against the concrete exterior.

Cris was within thirty feet of him when the man stopped, pivoted to his right, dived through a door-

way, and was gone — with the door slamming behind him. He looked back at Cris in the last second
before his face disappeared from view, and what
Cris saw made him shudder inside.

He was a young man of twenty or twenty-one.
His scraggly beard did nothing to hide his age, nor
could it conceal his sunken cheeks and dark, hol-
low-looking eyes. But all of those were secondary
observations — what Cris noticed first, and what
shocked him the most, was the look of abject terror
on the young man's face. Pure fear, tainted ever
so slightly by the desperate, you-won't-take-me-
alive look that comes into the eyes of a wild animal
when it is cornered and forced to fight for its life
against a foe it cannot hope to defeat.

Just as the man dived, Cris shouted "Stop!"
Maybe the word came too late, or maybe, judging
by the look on the man's face, he wasn't about to
heed the plea. As Cris bounded up to the door and
turned to face it, he could hear sounds of activity
from inside the building: the scraping of objects
being moved across the floor, dull thuds as those
objects were pushed against the metal door to
form a barricade. Then silence reigned again. Cris
stood still for a minute or so, trying to assess the
situation.

The people inside the building weren't doing
anything to give away their exact location; for all
Cris knew, they had moved into the building's
basement, onto an upper floor, or perhaps out of

the structure by a different exit — although that seemed unlikely, considering the trouble they had taken to make sure this door stayed closed.

"I must have scared the hell out of that guy," Cris mumbled. Then he recalled the part of his orders that prohibited him from making the first move toward any human being, and he immediately realized the reason for that instruction. "Of course . . . some of these people don't know what I am or who I am. They might think I'm —"

"Harrumph!" This sound came from in back of P-17, out of his field of vision.

Cris whirled and instinctively started to raise his right arm, but halted the movement when he saw a raggedy, hunched old man standing about fifteen feet away from him. The man was casually holding a pair of two-foot-long forceps in his left hand and looking at Cris with a gaze that was friendly and menacing at the same time.

"Who—"

"Shake," said the man, punctuating the word with a cackle of laughter. He stepped toward Cris and held out his right hand, apparently having interpreted Cris's gesture with his arm as one of friendliness. "Grayson's the name — Donald Grayson."

Cris didn't know what to do. One minute he was being looked at as a terrible monster by a man who seemed to know what he was doing, and the next he was being greeted by another man who, at first glance, didn't seem to have all his chips in the right sockets.

"Hello," Cris said reflexively as he lowered his right arm, feeling self-conscious. Now that he thought about it, he was pretty sure that his in-board computer would have prevented him from firing at the old man, but he was uncomfortable nonetheless about what he almost had done.

"Oh, not the sociable type, eh?" The man seemed amused rather than offended by Cris's re-fusal to shake his hand. "Can't blame you much — it's hard to know who your friends are these days. Maybe you could spare me a smile, and we'll take it from there."

"Sorry," Cris said, not caring to explain why he couldn't grant the man's request. "I'm not trying to be unfriendly. In fact, I'm very happy to see you, and—"

"How *do* you do that?" Grayson interrupted as he noticed that Cris's mouth didn't move when he spoke.

"Huh?"

"I can hear you talkin', but I can't *see* you talkin'. Saw a guy do that on the vid-ee-o a while back, but I never met anybody who was a real . . . ven-triloquist," he said, taking a second to search for the right word. "You got any other tricks?"

"Yeah, I could show you a thing or two," Cris muttered, suppressing a chuckle and feeling frus-trated at the same time. His first contact with someone from the outside world, and the guy turns out to be half-crazy — and maybe that was giving him too much credit. It was immediately obvious to Cris that Grayson was demented, or at least mentally ill, and he decided not to do anything to antagonize the old man.

"Whazzat?"

"I said, I'd rather know some things about you," Cris said in a friendly tone. "It's been a while since I've seen any other people. What are you doing? What's been going on up — around here?"

The old man started walking slowly back toward the street. Cris fell into step beside him, careful to keep his walking speed and the size of his stride down to match the man's pace. "Oh, things've been pretty quiet for the last week or so," he said offhandedly. "There was a lot o' runnin' around, yellin' and screamin', right at first — people and cars bouncin' around like balls in a box, all in a hurry and gettin' nowhere at the same time."

"Did the . . . the bugs come down here?"

"Bugs? Oh, you mean the gobblers. Naw, they didn't fall right here, not like I heard happened down south. Some of 'em wander in and out once in a while, but even an old guy like me can stay one step ahead of 'em if you just use your head," he said with a smile, tapping his temple with his right index finger. "School people are some o' the smartest people around, you know."

"I always thought so," said Cris, figuring his double meaning would be lost on Grayson. "But what have you been doing? Why are you still here?" He wanted to keep Grayson talking about himself, because he had a feeling that was the man's favorite subject.

"I didn't worry about the gobblers right away," Grayson said. "Nothin' an old man can do anyhow, and I figured the army'd have everything under control by Monday mornin'. So I stayed put at home — got a lot o' sleep after the power went out on Sunday — and came in to work just like usual the next day. Biggest traffic lock I ever saw — cars crawlin' along and people runnin' down the road right between them, actually goin' faster than the cars.

"I finally got off the big road, and it was easier to drive on the side streets — lots o' people, who'd get outta the way if you came at 'em fast enough, but not too many cars. I got to the high school — just a few blocks over that way, I'll show you — and what d' you think I saw?"

"What?" Cris asked obediently as they made a left turn and headed east, back along the same route he had taken originally.

"Nothin', that's what. No lights on, no people goin' in and out, no nothin'. It was like somebody decided there wasn't goin' to be any more school, just like that." That last statement came out in a tone that was a mixture of indignation and defeat. The old guy must have loved his work, Cris thought. And the man continued, "I went in, and the place was a wreck. What they didn't take, they busted up."

"Who's 'they'?"

"Oh, I dunno. Kids, I s'pose — smartasses who like t' break stuff just to see it busted. Maybe some adults, people lookin' for things they could steal and use. What's it matter?" Grayson snapped, angry at having his monologue interrupted.

"I guess it docsn't."

"You betcha," said the old man, not awed in the least by the fact that his traveling companion was nearly eight feet tall, attired in nothing but armored skin, and radiating as much heat as a small campfire. Cris, who didn't want to risk being scolded twice, let the old man tell his story without another interruption as they shuffled and sizzled their way along the road.

Grayson had been — still considered himself to be — a school custodian. When he found his place of work, a place he loved even more than his home, ravaged and ruined, he decided to become a self-appointed guardian of what little was left to guard. It was at this point, Cris conjectured, that something inside the man must have snapped. His only purpose in life was to keep the school clean and equipped to hold classes. He was determined to hold the fort until everything got back to normal and students once again started filing into the classrooms and laboratories.

He scavenged a few pieces of still-usable furniture and set up living quarters for himself in a third-floor laboratory. He had enough presence of mind not to clean things up too much, so that intruders wouldn't realize anyone was living in the building. When someone did venture inside, which wasn't often, Grayson would hide in a stairwell or a closet and wait until he was alone again. "I'm no fool," he said, sounding as if he was trying to convince himself as much as Cris. "Let 'em come, let 'em go — I'll stay right where I belong, and when all this blows over they won't have to go lookin' for old Don Grayson. Haven't missed a day of work in forty-three years, and I'm not gonna start now."

But classes aren't in session, Cris thought, and almost verbalized that statement before he caught himself. No sense in pointing out the obvious; at best it would get him another reprimand, and at worst it might bring out some sort of extreme emotional reaction that would really put the old man over the edge.

As they came within sight of the school, Cris asked about the forceps the man was carrying. Grayson held up the instrument proudly, referred to it as his "extractor," and without saying it in so many words managed to convey that he used the tool when he went scavenging, to pluck edible and usable tidbits out of garbage piles and refuse containers. "Always been a clean person," he said pridefully, the words sounding strange coming from a face sporting a growth of scraggly white beard, on top of a scrawny frame dressed in clothing that probably hadn't been next to a tube of detergent for weeks.

Grayson had been on a "shopping trip," as he called it, when he ran into Cris. "Haven't been real far away from home lately, but food's gettin' harder and harder to find around here. Not much to show for the last couple hours, but then again I've been talkin' when I should've been workin'. . . . Whoa! Hold it there!"

Cris noticed the person ahead and off to their left in the same instant that Grayson had shouted those words. A nondescript, middle-aged man perhaps a head taller than Grayson had appeared from around the corner of a building and was bending over what looked like a pile of refuse and garbage.

"I saw that pile first, and I was on my way to it," Grayson said menacingly as he moved closer to the man, brandishing his forceps in his left hand. Cris fell into step slightly behind him, ambling along to keep up with Grayson's trotting pace but careful not to overtake him.

"You hold it," the other man shot back as he stood up straight. He looked desperate and angry, desperate enough that he apparently was not intimidated by the appearance of either Grayson or P-17. Grayson didn't slacken his pace, and when he was just a few steps away he slipped his right hand inside his coat and pulled out a small projectile revolver — more than sufficient to kill a man at close range.

Cris and the scavenger both froze as Grayson halted about five feet away from the man with the pistol aimed directly at his face.

"Is it loaded?" asked the man with a quaver in his voice as he thrust his hands over his head.

"Wanna find out?" Grayson delivered the answer like he had been practicing it, or as though he had used the line before.

Cris took in the scene before him as if it was being played out in slow motion. Although only seconds had passed since the encounter had begun, he knew he should have done something by now. But what?

He immediately dismissed trying to use his weaponry; even if he could have fired at Grayson to prevent him from using his gun, he didn't want to risk killing the old man. He thought about trying to grab Grayson's arm, but wasn't sure he could do it in time to keep him from pulling the trigger. Should he leap forward, push the other man out of the way, and take the bullet himself? He might hurt the guy by knocking him down, but that was better than . . .

Cris opened his arms, lowered his shoulders, tensed his leg muscles, and sprang forward. . . .

. . . but instead of lunging out and shoving the man out of the way, his body simply froze in place!

Out of power? Cris thought. No, that's impossible — I can still see and hear and—

"No!" Cris shouted as he watched, frozen and helpless, while Grayson's finger tightened on the trigger. He yelled the word again, but it was drowned out by the sharp crack of a gunshot. Cris instinctively took a step backward and straightened up, discovering much to his amazement that he could move again.

The man took the bullet just above his eyes, causing him to fall backward. He probably was dead by the time his body hit the ground, and certainly was lifeless when Cris knelt over him a couple of seconds later. He knew immediately that he could do nothing for the man.

As Cris rose and turned toward Grayson, the old man was lowering the gun and taking a careful step backward. The revolver was pointing down, but the arm holding it was still tensed. "Now you know — the gun *is* loaded," said Grayson snappishly. "So don't get any closer to this stuff or I'll give you one in the head, too."

"I won't touch the . . . stuff," Cris said, hoping the old man would calm down.

"*My* stuff," Grayson said, trying to keep one eye on P-17 and one eye on the pile. "Don't expect there's anything left here anyway," he said matter-of-factly. "But if there is, I'm gonna get it."

Cris stood and stared at Grayson for a few seconds while his mind tried to assess what he could

— should? — do next. Then Grayson's curiosity, or desperation, got the better of him. He stopped watching Cris, stooped down, cackled softly to himself, and began lifting and moving pieces of snow-covered rubbish with his forceps.

Cris watched for another second. Then P-17 silently turned and headed for home.

23

For the first few hours after he returned underground, no one spoke to Cris except to give him curt instructions while he underwent a thorough biological, mechanical, and electronic examination. As part of the process, the record of his mission that had been stored in his internal computer was downloaded — but the memories in his organic brain were his to keep. Judging from the self-satisfied comments of the various technicians who took part in the testing, Cris assumed his body had come back from his first mission in perfect condition — which should come as no surprise to them, he said to himself, since they wouldn't let me do anything.

Then he was left alone in a room, and two minutes later Traynor came through the door.

"Not a bad test drive," he said amiably. "Got a couple of hours to spare?"

"I . . . I suppose," said Cris, not sure what to make of the question.

"Good." Traynor's voice was drier and more even now. "It might take that long for me to go through your performance analysis."

"I just had—"

"That was a physical analysis. This is different."

"In other words—"

"In other words, I'm here to discuss the performance of your most important body part — that lump of tissue between your shoulder blades. We're going to talk about what *you* did."

"My report card," Cris said a little glumly. Then, sarcastically, "Did I pass?"

"Well . . . you did get back alive." The combination of acid and wryness in the man's voice stopped Cris from responding right away, and Traynor used the pause to get his lecture started.

"You have been told time and time again," he said with condescension, "that conservation of power is vital to your continued existence. The charge in your batteries is like blood — you've only got a certain amount of it, and when it's gone, you're gone."

"I don't get it. What did—"

"Just listen. By the time I'm done, all of your questions will be answered."

Cris kept quiet, and for the next hour Traynor

treated him to an amazingly detailed rehash of his mission. The internal computer's data-storage mechanism was more thorough than he had imagined; the only thing it couldn't record, apparently, was his thoughts — but sometimes the computer came dangerously close to doing even that.

He learned, among many other things, that it was not necessary for him to use his sonic transmitters to find his way along the tunnel; all he had to do was point his feet in the direction he wanted to go and lock his leg joints into straight-ahead orientation so that he wouldn't weave from side to side. What he did cost him twenty times more power than he would have expended by simply putting one foot in front of the other.

It was utterly foolish of him to generate excessive body heat the way he did. He used fifty times as much power as he needed to merely keep his mechanics and hydraulics from stiffening up, and, in Traynor's words, he "left a trail that an unconscious blind man could have followed."

His sprint down the street after the stranger was a tactical blunder for a couple of reasons. He wasted power by going into ultraspeed mode when he didn't have to, and wasted time by overshooting his destination. And — as Cris already knew — he had committed an error by trying to chase and catch the young man in the first place. Well, "committed an error" wasn't exactly the way Traynor put it. . . .

"You are the first recruit I've trained who ever disobeyed that order on his first trip outside. A precedent-setting example of bad judgment." For the first time in Traynor's monologue, the man's expression and tone of voice both turned steely cold.

While one part of his brain considered the absurdity of a much smaller man — without any "military devices" at all — talking to him in a threatening, insulting tone, Cris's better half told him to keep quiet. Traynor let his last words and the atmosphere they created in the room sink in for a few seconds. When he finally relaxed his posture and cleared his throat, Cris let out a cerebral sigh of relief.

"And now we get to the good part," Traynor continued.

Oh boy, thought Cris. Here it comes. . . .

"You did a remarkable job handling that old man Grayson." Traynor smiled as he said that, and in the next few minutes Cris came to realize that he had said "good" because he *meant* it!

The old man, Traynor explained, was not unfamiliar. In fact, through some sort of weird sixth sense or blind, dumb luck, Grayson had voluntarily encountered other Cyborg Commandos on two previous occasions — which helped explain to Cris why the old man had not been taken aback by his appearance.

Traynor told Cris that the man apparently had

thought the other two cyborgs were robots, not so much because of the way they looked but because of the way they sounded; they had not been equipped with the voice simulator that had been installed in P-17's body. But because Cris had a real voice, the doctor apparently figured him for a human being, conveniently disregarding all the nonhuman things about his body.

"To put it charitably," Traynor summarized, "the man is not rational."

"I could see that right away," said Cris.

"Obviously," Traynor said warmly, "or you never would have handled him the way you did."

"Right," Cris said. "He seemed like he was on edge."

"Exactly. The worst way to deal with people like him is to be forceful, or irritate them by abandoning them. Go along with them, don't do anything to get them excited, and wait for them to lose interest. The other two cyborgs who've encountered him didn't have as much patience as you did."

"What happened with the others?" Cris asked.

"P-12, about a week ago, tried to ignore the guy, simply walked away, and that sent Grayson into a frenzy. We didn't know at the time that he had a gun — maybe he didn't, then — but I wouldn't be surprised to find out that he took out his anger on the next person, or the next few people, he met.

"Then, three days ago, he befriended P-14 for a

while, the same way he latched onto you. Everything was going fine until P-14 decided to help him by lifting a crate so Grayson could see what was under it. Grayson saw that as an attempt to steal 'his stuff,' and the good samaritan came back with a bullet in his right arm."

"I assumed the gun was loaded," Cris offered.

"You figured right. You played it the way you should have."

"But I tried—"

"You tried to take a direct hand in what was happening, and at that instant your inboard computer took over. Your . . . programming . . . wouldn't let you throw your body at the man, which was just as well. You might have killed him, and almost certainly would have injured him, by doing that. At best, you would have angered Grayson by making that kind of move, and then you and the other man would have both ended up getting shot."

So what did I do *right*? Cris thought. As if he was answering that unspoken question, Traynor continued.

"You could have done a lot of things instead of what you tried to do," the man said, "and it's to your credit that you dismissed those other alternatives."

What alternatives?

"You could have made some sort of move not directed at either of the men, something designed to distract Grayson and give the other man a chance to get away. Again, all that would have accomplished would be to turn Grayson against you and infuriate him. The last thing we want is for that old man to get really agitated and go on a wild, indiscriminate shooting spree."

In fact, Cris had not even considered doing something to affect the situation indirectly — but he wasn't about to let Traynor know that. He had begun to see what Traynor was getting at, and he was upset and discouraged by the conclusion he had come to.

"In other words," Cris said with resignation, "I'm helpless when it comes to keeping one man from killing another one."

"That's not exactly right, but close," Traynor said. "The point is that you could not control whether that man lived or died. Incidents like the one you witnessed are going on all the time up there — people are surviving the best way they know how, and other people are paying the price for that."

"But how can I just stand by and let people murder each other?"

"We need you to help save the world, P-17. We're not asking you to change it."

24

They let Cris rest a bit longer than usual, simply by reprogramming his internal computer so that it fed sleep-inducing chemicals to his brain for five hours instead of four. Knowing his history as a slow riser, they gave his brain a full one and one-half hours to get itself working in high gear.

The men who gave the orders authorized these things because they were the only two ways in which they could offer Cris Holman anything that resembled physical pleasure. They wanted to make him feel good, to the limited extent that they could accomplish this, because they were about to ask — no, require — Cris Holman to risk his life.

Traynor came into Cris's room an hour and fifteen minutes after he had been awakened. The man made casual, animated conversation for a few

minutes, as though he was feeling Cris out, checking for residual effects of what had happened on
his first outing the day before. He discovered, to
his relief, that the brain inside P-17 was feeling
anything but discouraged or even subdued.

"You feeling okay?"

"I always feel okay. That's one of the fringe
benefits — one of the few fringe benefits — of
being wrapped up in this silly suit."

"You know what I mean."

"Yeah, Traynor, I know what you mean."

"I was concerned about your mental state, not
your physical condition." Traynor took a deep
breath. "We're sending you out again today."

"Boy, you sure know how to ease into a subject.
What do I get to do today, walk to the store for a
loaf of soybread?"

"Not exactly . . ."

* * *

It was late morning, Cris guessed. The sky was
only lightly overcast, about as bright as it got these
days. The weather had calmed down considerably
since the terrible climatic outburst that preceded
and accompanied the alien invasion, but this part
of the country still had at least a decent-sized
snowstorm about every third day. Fortunately, from
all appearances, today was not going to be one of
those days.

Cris was on a sweep of the far east sector of the area near the base, one of two Cyborg Commando units engaged in this particular operation. They were a team, but a team whose members — if they did their jobs properly — would not see each other until the sweep was finished.

Their routes had been carefully orchestrated so that every street, every alleyway in the area would be traversed by both of them, but with a lapse of at least several minutes between each visitation. The methodology was very similar to that used by police when they set traps for drivers who thought that ninety miles per hour was not a sufficiently liberal speed limit. You might see Trafficop Number One, conspicuously positioned on his jet-scooter, in time to slow down before he could track on you . . . or, he might let you go anyway and get you thinking that today was your lucky day. So you push up the booster a bit, figuring you've just had your first and last brush with the law — and the next thing you know, five miles down the road, Trafficop Number Two pulls out from alongside a building and brings you down faster than you can say "Er . . . My speedometer must be broken."

Cris was playing the part of Number One, making no attempt at stealth as he plodded casually along his prescribed route. He was bait, in one sense of the word, but bait that could bite back if given a chance. His primary purpose was to attract the attention of any creatures that might be in the area, drawing them out of hiding so that Number Two, a more experienced commando, could blast or burn them out of existence. But Cris's orders did allow him to take the initiative and use his own weaponry if he found himself in what Traynor had called "an obvious life-threatening situation."

"And just what do you consider obvious?"

"That's a decision you have to make, based on the circumstances you encounter. That's why—"

"I know. . . . That's why I have a brain."

"What I was going to say is, that's why the orders can't be any more specific. But I guess it boils down to the same thing."

He was about six blocks east of the access bay, on the perimeter of the area he was patrolling, when Cris saw a dead body. It was that of a middle-aged man, perhaps fifty or fifty-five, who was huddled in a fetal position just outside the basement door of an old-style house, the kind covered in cheap aluminum panels that were meant to (but never did) look like moss-covered brick.

Once he got over his initial surprise, the sight didn't bother Cris. He had seen corpses earlier in Whitewater, and a few here in Manitowoc when he first arrived in the city, and a lot of them had been more gruesome to behold than the pitiful figure before his eyes at the moment. It was impossible to tell if the man had died from starvation or exposure, but it clearly had not been a violent or a painful death. He looked as though he had simply decided to lie down, perhaps knowing as he did it that he would never get up again.

The body was about three-quarters covered by snow, and the man was dressed in white, so that even the exposed portion wasn't easily visible from more than a few yards away. That, thought Cris, was probably what had saved him from being discovered before now. Discovered, and . . . . He tried to blot the last part of that thought out of his mind.

He got an idea. Something his orders didn't expressly permit him to do, but didn't expressly prohibit, either. Cris pondered briefly whether or not to put his plan into action, but the effort was really just an exercise in formality. As soon as the idea came to him, he had decided to follow it through.

Cris picked the body up out of the snow and walked out to the street. He laid it down beside the curb, then turned his back on it and resumed his stroll. He took a left turn at the end of the block, walked a few more paces to get behind the edge of the building that stood on the corner, and then took off at a fast trot around the building and through an alleyway that ran behind the houses and shops facing the street. He doubled back to a spot where he could keep the body under surveillance. With one step he could move out and fire at anything that approached it. If the next moving thing he saw was the other member of his team, he might get in a lot of trouble for not following orders. But if it was something else . . .

Cris willed his auditory receptors to become super-sensitive, and his brain was immediately assailed by a constant, low whooshing noise — the sound of the wind — frequently augmented by a whispering rustle as the breeze picked up a small patch of frozen snow and pushed the granules around. He got accustomed to those sounds within a few seconds and effectively tuned them out (although he could still hear them) while he waited, poised, for any other sonic vibration that would break the pattern.

Five tension-filled minutes later, he heard something else — a shuffle, as though something was being dragged across the ground; a slight wheeze, and a gentle thump. Then . . . nothing. Ten seconds later, the same three sounds were repeated, and Cris got a fix on their location: to his right, up the street, about a hundred and twenty feet away. The noises were distorted, not quite pure, as though they were bouncing off a solid surface before reaching his ears. From this bit of information, Cris deduced that they were coming from between a couple of buildings.

The sounds came with increasing frequency and regularity, until the next shuffle was right on the heels of, and sometimes overlapping with, the last thump. Something was moving, in a very unhuman fashion, in Cris's direction. He fought off the urge to step out and get the jump on whatever was approaching, because his ears told him that the sound was still not reaching him directly, and if he revealed himself too soon he might lose the advantage of surprise.

Then, suddenly, the sounds became louder and more sharply defined, and Cris sensed that once he stepped out from his hiding place, there would be nothing but empty air between him and the object of his attention. The noise continued to increase in volume as its source drew closer and closer, advancing toward the body in the snow and toward the unseen enemy that was lying in wait.

Cris stood it as long as he could, until his head seemed to pound under the onslaught of the amplified vibrations. Then he switched his hearing back to normal human sensitivity, and the change to near-silence startled him for an instant. All he could hear now was the repeated thumping sound, and instead of booming like a drum it resembled the sound of a fist punching a cushion. But the sound was definitely there, and definitely still getting closer.

He took a couple of seconds to calm himself down and think through what he was about to do — and then he did it.

Cris leaped and whirled at the same time, coming down six feet away from where he had stood concealed around the corner of a building and facing directly into the path of a . . . a thing! In the same instant that he landed, he brought his right arm up into the firing position. Two searing beams of light shot out of his knuckles, and a fraction of a millisecond later they struck the monster in the up-thrust center section of its elongated body.

The appearance of the creature took Cris by surprise. Unlike the others he had seen, it vaguely resembled a giant caterpillar, both in how it looked and how it was moving. Even as it took the laser hit, it continued to come forward, the front section rising up as the center section dropped back toward the ground. By pushing its rear section forward (shuffle), elevating its center section (wheeze), and then simultaneously dropping the center section (thump) and raising its front to propel the "head" in the desired direction, it had moved from its own place of seclusion to a location about one hundred feet away from the dead body and about one hundred twenty feet from where Cris now stood.

Cris saw the twin laser beams come out the other side of the creature's convoluted body just before they shut off. He did not call for another burst, automatically assuming that no living thing could survive such an attack. He was wrong.

The thing was affected by the laser blast, but it was far from dead. Soundlessly, except for the noise made by its body scraping and bumping against the ground, the creature reared up and began to twist away from Cris, moving more quickly than it seemed capable of doing.

Its first instinct seemed to be to turn and run, to

get away from the man-thing that had hurt it. Cris's initial impulse was the opposite. He wanted revenge — he wanted to kill.

"You're dead, you bastard!" He bounded forward, closing to within about fifty feet of the creature's left flank. Then, just before he started raising his arm to fire again, the thing turned its head around and lurched right at him!

Cris froze, for an eternity that lasted all of five seconds, as he got his first good look at what passed for the creature's head. Two mandibles clicked together convulsively, and the flesh (if that's what it was) around them stretched and pulsed obscenely with each movement. The cavity between the mandibles was not a mouth, really — more like simply a deep hollow in the thing's body, deep enough to contain a human body while it was suffocated and then, somehow, digested. The monster had no features that were obviously eyes, yet it seemed to be able to find its way around, and it definitely knew exactly where Cris was located.

"The thing suckered me in!" Cris thought as a wave of anger and desperation snapped him out of his momentary shock. He leveled his forearm for another laser blast — a long, single one this time — and as the beam shot out of his knuckle, he pivoted his arm through a small arc. Instead of punching one small hole through the creature, this shot cut a slicing path, starting at one side of the tubular body and searing across its breadth.

The beam only lasted for a second, but that was time enough to chop the alien into two pieces. A six-foot length of grayish-white pulp, the head section, fell with a splat, hitting the snow-packed street about twenty feet in front of Cris and slightly off to his right.

What he saw next was even more horrifying than the sight of the whole creature bearing down on him. The severed section was still alive! The mandibles kept working, the mouth-hole continued to pulse, and the outer surface of the body contracted and stretched. The head was trying to keep itself moving along the ground, but without the leverage provided by the rest of its body, the thing couldn't move more than a few inches on each thrust.

Sensing that he was in no immediate danger from the still-active but essentially immobile head section, Cris took a couple of steps to where he could see the cross-section of the creature's insides that the laser had exposed. Another shock — the thing didn't seem to *have* any insides! It was solid all the way through beneath the thin, hard outer layer of its body, and the interior seemed to be composed entirely of a sickly, gray pulp. Most of the surface of the wound was blackened, no doubt charring from the heat of the laser. The interior pulp glistened in several spots and appeared to be slowly oozing some kind of clear liquid, but Cris got the impression that the thing was not exactly bleeding to death. He wondered if the laser actually had cauterized the wound at the same time it caused it.

During the few seconds it had taken Cris to make all these observations, the rear body section had lain inert, trailing diagonally across the street like a monstrous, lifeless worm. He gave it only a passing notice, assuming that since he had disconnected the "brain," the body wouldn't be any further threat. Then the twenty-foot-long, decapitated worm began to twitch . . . to move.

"The dying gasp," Cris muttered to himself, briefly startled by the movement but then successfully convincing himself that the motions were involuntary. He stood and watched, quite satisfied with himself, even while the convulsions got stronger instead of weaker. "Any second now the whole thing is going to just collapse," he said. The thing began to heave and thrash, buckling and whirling irregularly, unpredictably, and even more rapidly than the creature had moved when it was whole.

"It's still not dead!" Cris breathed, amazed and a little afraid. "Die!" he screamed. "Die, you son of a bitch!" He drew another bead on the writhing mass of pulp, aiming for the midpoint of the cylindrical bulk and intending to slice it into two halves, which he hoped would be easier to handle. He aimed, he shot . . .

. . . and he missed.

Because the area he had targeted on was moving perpendicular to his plane of fire, the thing's body shifted just enough in the fraction of a second between aiming and firing so that Cris's sweep-beam went sizzling right past it. The light continued on a downward path until it hit the street about fifteen feet away, instantly sending up an enormous cloud of steam from the snow that it vaporized on contact.

The thrashing tube of pulp seemed to have no sense about it. Cris realized he wasn't being attacked, at least not purposefully. So, shaken by his miscalculation and the missed shot that resulted from it, he simply stared at the thing from a safe distance as it flopped and wriggled. "Maybe it'll just burn itself out," he said, groping for something to be hopeful about.

And then, to Cris's amazement, the body *did* begin to burn!

More precisely, it popped and sizzled, first at the tail end that was most distant from Cris and then at about the midpoint of the body, the place where his errant laser-beam shot had been aimed. "But I didn't . . ." he mumbled, just before he noticed what — no, who! — was causing the thing to blister and bubble.

His unexpected help had come from another Cyborg Commando, the trailing member of Cris's team. His companion was about half a block away, walking briskly toward the monster's body with both arms extended in front of his body, palms out. In a flash, Cris realized that his teammate — his savior — was using his microwave projectors to literally cook the senseless but still dangerous creature.

Cris backed away as the other commando approached, not eager to find out what would happen if he got in the way of one of the invisible, high-intensity blasts of radiation.

The other man — Cris still used that word, automatically — moved his arms slowly from side to side as he advanced, so that the radiation would come in contact with as much of the thing's body as possible. Within fifteen seconds the headless body was all but motionless in the street. Its flesh was bubbling and smoking along most of its length and giving off an unearthly stench that made Cris cut off his olfactory sensors for the time being. The man continued to walk in his general direction, but now he lowered his arms slightly and turned his fingers downward, apparently directing the radiation along the lower edge of the wormlike body. The thing seemed to be melting, collapsing where it lay, as gravity caused the upper part to fall into the sizzling puddle beneath it.

Suddenly feeling sheepish at not having contributed to the kill, Cris turned and trained his own microwave projectors on the head section that continued to twitch ineffectually several yards away from where he stood. He called up a full-power, narrow-beam shot of radiation from each palm — and most definitely hit what he aimed at this time.

A fraction of a second after the beams hit the head, the target exploded with an obscene squishing sound, spraying everything in a fifty-foot radius — including Commando P-17 — with hot, oozing globs of dead monster flesh.

The fact that Cris couldn't smell the stuff that covered him and dripped off his body didn't keep him from being utterly revolted by what had happened, so disgusted and mentally nauseated that he forgot all about being embarrassed. He raised an index finger and wiped away a bit of stuff that was partially obscuring his left eye, then instinctively wiped his hands down his face and across his upper body, trying to scrape off as much of the goo as he could.

"No matter how much of that stuff you get rid of, you're still going to need a cleaning when we get back."

The voice came from the man who was approaching Cris, brushing his palms against each other in a parody of someone who has just finished a dirty job.

"What . . . what did I do?" asked Cris, unable to think of anything more intelligent at the moment.

"Just overcooked it a little, that's all. Gets the job done just the same, but it leaves quite a mess for the regular army guys to clean up — and it gives you a rather severe case of body odor, too."

"Sorry . . ."

"Hell, you don't have to apologize to me. I turned off my sniffer before I got too close," Cris's companion said. "Tell it to the technicians back in the sanitation department."

"Did . . . did we do okay?" he stuttered, still at a loss for words.

"Well, we got us a bug, and that was the whole idea of this little excursion. Maybe we didn't do it by the book, but I was never much of a reader anyway."

"You're not mad?"

"Why should I be mad? I feel as fit as a micro-chip, it's a beautiful day, and we just cooked a caterpillar. If you were a military man like me, you'd know that a soldier in wartime has only two responsibilities. Number one is kill the enemy. Number two is stay alive so you can keep doing number one. That bug is definitely dead, and you and I are definitely alive, in spite of what you look like. So—"

"How do you know I'm not a military man?" Cris interrupted.

"Well, let's just say I took the trouble to find out a little about you before I decided to trust you with my life."

"Well, I don't know anything about you — and apparently," said Cris, gesturing at his own torso, "I have a lot of other things to learn, too."

"Well, we have at least that much in common.

My assumed name is C-12. Pleased to meet you, P-17 — or can I call you Cris?"

"You know that too, huh? Sure, you can call me Cris — if I can call you . . .?"

"Call me John." Cris couldn't see the smile on C-12's face, but he could hear it in John's voice. "C'mon," his companion added. "It's time to head back and get you cleaned up."

As they walked back toward the nearest accessway to the underground complex, Cris asked John a lot of questions. The other man answered every one, occasionally volunteering extra information. But sometimes his answers were more perplexing than no answer at all.

Was it a good idea to bring the dead body out into the street for bait?

"Oh, that's where the guy came from. Hard to tell if it helped or not. Sometimes they go after dead meat, but they seem to much prefer the living, moving kind. More likely, that bug was just out for an afternoon crawl, and we got lucky."

Why didn't his laser blast kill the thing?

"The bugs don't have guts like you and me — or like we used to have, anyway. You can hurt 'em by cutting 'em in half or burning holes through 'em, but to make sure they die you have to blast the whole body."

And that's what the microwave projectors are for?

"The cookers are good, especially at short

range, but it takes a while to learn just how much power to use, and how wide a beam you need. Your mistake — or break it into two mistakes, if you want — was using too much heat and too thin a beam. Don't worry, you'll get the hang of it — or else you'll be using up a lot of disinfectant."

How did he and John get teamed up for this mission?

"I asked for you."

Why?

"Age has its privileges. I can team up with any new civvie I want."

No, why *him*?

"Well, I told someone I'd keep an eye on you — figuratively speaking, of course."

Someone? Who?

"I am not at liberty to reveal that information. In civilian terms, it's none of your business."

Why not?

"Look, you're not a dumb kid. So don't ask any more dumb questions." John's tone was friendly but firm. And since they were now about to enter the accessway, Cris didn't ask any more questions at all.

25

February 15, 2035

As his brain sank down into sleep, Cris reflected on how he might remember his first complete week as a full-fledged Cyborg Commando. It had been a time of emotional extremes, and he wasn't sure which feelings would become uppermost in his memory.

He hoped he would never forget the supreme satisfaction, the ecstasy of demolishing and disintegrating the loathsome creatures that killed the people he loved. The novelty of this job isn't going to wear off too quickly, Cris thought as he smiled to himself.

He didn't want to remember the times between combat missions when he had felt sad, lonely, and insecure, but he couldn't keep those memories and those feelings from coming over him. He was also troubled by the mysterious answer his new partner had given when Cris asked why John had teamed up with him. *Who*, Cris wondered, had asked a perfect stranger to keep an eye on him? He hoped, as he had for each of the last several days before falling asleep, that John would say something to solve this mystery, which was bothering Cris more and more.

Cris fell into a restless sleep, full of uncertainty and confusion.

* * *

"Don't ask me how, but I can tell something's troubling you."

"Aw, what gave it away? My maniacal gaze? My wrinkled nose? My clenched teeth?"

"Come on, John. Tell me about it." Nora's tone was gentle, but her observation had been a serious one and she was expecting the same kind of response.

Nora Whitaker had become visibly more relaxed and more cheerful over the last few days. Cris was everything the technicians had said he would be — sharp reflexes, dependable instincts, brisk and accurate reasoning. Although every CC's brain possessed all of these talents, a few Commandos were truly exceptional, and Cris was one of those. He was still young and inexperienced, but no one held that against him. As one techno wrote at the bottom of an evaluation sheet, "The better he gets, the better he's going to get."

Nora had come through shock, numbness, and horrible anxiety to a point where she was getting accustomed to — almost comfortable with — having a son with a cybernetic body. A son who didn't know she existed. No one but John knew her secret, she had made him swear to keep it to himself, and she had no intention of telling anyone else.

"You've got to talk to Cris." John Edwards was not the type to hold his tongue once he had decided to use it. Nora had suspected what his problem was, so his words came as no real surprise. And she did want to help him feel better, but . . . she caught a small part of herself wishing that she had not pressed the issue.

"John, I've been over it all in my mind more than you have. Cris is better off not knowing who his mother is, or even that his mother is alive. After everything else he's been through, I don't want to risk him . . . . He's already lost me once."

"You can't carry around a secret like yours and keep yourself in one piece psychologically, especially when you see your son every day," John urged patiently.

"Who are you to be lecturing me about psychology?" Nora asked, a little edgily. John had come close to touching a nerve. She picked up a glass of ice water and sipped it, using the time to calm herself. "I'm getting used to the way things are —

the way things have to be. Cris has been doing brilliantly with you, and I don't get nearly as nervous any more when the two of you go out to . . . outside together."

"Superficially, you're a helluva lot better," John said. "But there's some anxiety and regret down inside that won't go away by itself."

"Don't tell me—"

He interrupted her with an argument he had never used before, a fresh note of urgency in his voice. "He *knows* there's something I'm not telling him, and it's driving both of us crazy. I can't relax around him because if I do, I might let something slip — that's almost happened a couple of times already. And because of that, he can't relax around me. He thinks I'm keeping bad news from him, and he's curious and hurt and angry all at once. If the big bosses downstairs knew what was going on, they wouldn't let us keep teaming together."

"I need you to stay with him, John. For a while longer at least." Nora couldn't keep from panicking a little, even though John's words were not said as a threat.

"I'm not going to tell anyone, and I'm not going to ask for a reassignment," he said tenderly. "All I'm trying to say is that the problem, the . . . distance . . . between me and Cris isn't going to go away unless we, or you, do something about it."

"John, please—"

The videocommunicator in Nora's office beeped

softly. By the way she quickly, eagerly turned her attention to the machine, it was obvious to John that she wouldn't be pressed into pursuing the subject any further.

"I have to . . ." she said, looking briefly from the screen to John's face.

"I know. Duty calls," said John. "We'll finish this talk some other time, okay?" He stood, briskly, as the question came out.

Nora had time to respond before John turned and left the room, but all she could bring herself to give him was a silent wave.

* * *

Once they learned what they would be up against this time, John Edwards and Cris Holman knew that their minds would have to be just as finely tuned, just as quick and powerful as their bodies. They both gave their unswerving attention to every word of the short briefing:

"Yesterday one unit reported the long-range sighting of an invader that seemed to have unnatural protrusions on its body, but P-13 did not investigate or pursue because of low power readings. Six hours ago, *two* units were damaged in an encounter with a creature that was . . . somehow . . . holding and operating a launcher for explosive fragmentation grenades.

"Two invaders of similar description were sight-

ed less than thirty minutes ago by army reconnais-
sance in sector 31, heading directly east. Start at
the lakefront, work your way inland, and stop
them."

Creatures carrying weapons . . . . Cris and John
both tossed that thought around in their minds for a
second, and then the veteran spoke first.

"Well, kid, it looks like bug-plugging has taken
on some extra added significance."

"I was just thinking the same thing," said Cris in
an equally jaunty tone. He was concerned, but not
afraid. These were the good times — the times
when he and John did together what they did best.
He was much more comfortable being in combat
with C-12 than he was in a one-on-one conversation with John Edwards.

"It was getting too easy, anyway," John said.
"We need a challenge, right, partner?"

"Right," Cris agreed readily.

When C-12 and P-17 left the base to carry out
their orders, all of the on-duty personnel (and
many of those who were off-duty) would have their
faces glued to monitor screens from the beginning
to the end of this mission. The best soldiers man
could create were about to have their first purposeful encounter with invaders that were . . . somehow
. . . armed.

26

February 15, 2035

It was a lousy way to travel.

Crrrunchhh . . .

With his sensors turned up to maximum efficiency, Cris heard every vibrating, ear-splitting step that P-17 took as he and John loped along at a speed five times faster than a human being could run.

Boom!

As his feet broke through the soft snow cover and impacted gently with the ground or pavement beneath, each noise sounded to Cris as though someone was operating a grindstone, and then a huge drum, right next to his ear.

It was essential, for the times between steps, that John and Cris have their auditory receptors turned up. They wanted to be able to hear any strange noises before whatever was making those noises could detect their presence, but they had to get where they were going in a hurry, and that meant suffering through the *crunch-boom-crunch* in the meantime.

Cris was glad when John pulled up at an intersection and took a few seconds to scout around. "The sound of our running is making my head split," he whispered. "How are we ever going to sneak up on anything?"

"We aren't making *that* much noise," John breathed back. "Try not to be so sensitive, kid."

"Right," said Cris, acknowledging the joke. "But we have to—"

"This way. I think I see a good hiding place just down the street."

With Cris on his heels scanning their flanks, John paced eastward for about a block until they came to the entrance of one of the biggest buildings for blocks around, ten floors high and at least twice as tall as any of the structures near it.

"After you," John said, gesturing for Cris to precede him inside.

"What? *We're* going to hide? When you said 'hiding place,' I thought you meant—"

"We're not running away from anything, we're just taking the high ground. If those things come anywhere within a half-mile of this building, we'll have the drop on them."

"And if they don't?"

"Then we try another lookout post. Come on, get in and go up."

Cris ducked through the doorway and sprang up the inside stairways as quickly as he could, exiting onto the flat rooftop with John on his heels. They didn't want to be inside any longer than necessary, because — no matter how sensitive their hearing was — the sound of approaching enemies might not be detectable through the concrete walls of the building.

They stationed themselves at diagonally opposite corners of the rooftop, careful to stay low and next to the two-foot-high barrier that surrounded the edge of the roof. They trained their cybernetic eyes and ears on the battered, desolate urban terrain below them. John, scanning the area farthest from the lake, was the first to detect something strange.

"Psst!" John whispered, gesturing for Cris to join him.

Running in a half-crouch, Cris got across the roof to his companion as quickly as he could. "What is it?" he asked, just as his ears picked up the sound John had heard.

It was faint and irregular, but unmistakable — the same shuffling sound Cris had first heard just more than a month ago. The same relentless, plodding, scraping sound that the unearthly invaders made as they moved.

"One of them, maybe more, off that way," John

said, indicating an area to the west and slightly south of the building they were on.

"Reverberating, like the noises are being reflected off something on the way to us," Cris added. It was not the first time he had heard that kind of sound.

"Yeah, pretty smart," John responded. Then Cris realized John wasn't referring to him. "They know they could be seen easily from this vantage point," he continued, "so they're keeping to the trenches — the alleys, maybe the spaces between buildings — as long as they can."

After only a few seconds of listening, both John and Cris had accurate fixes on the source of the sound. It was louder now, and it got so loud in the following couple of minutes that Cris adjusted his auditory receptors to normal (human) sensitivity — he had been through this sequence of events before — and found that he could still track on the sound with ease. "You can turn your hearing down now," he whispered to John.

"Thanks," John said at normal volume. "I just did."

"Shhhh!"

"Aw, don't worry. They can't hear our voices from this far away. If I were you — and I almost am — I'd be more concerned about them detecting all the radio signals and magnetic waves we're putting out. If they've got weapons, maybe they've got weapon *finders*, too."

"What a pleasant thought. So, what do we do now? Wait for them to make the first move?"

"They're already making it. Now just get behind me and be patient." John sounded tense, curt.

"Behind you? What can I do behind you?"

"You can stay out of trouble and keep yourself in one piece. Now get *down!*"

John had never pulled rank on him so vehemently, never given him that kind of a . . . command . . . before. He had to obey, but he didn't have to like it.

"I can take care of myself," he grumbled. Then, "I don't need you to watch out for me this way." John ignored both statements, and Cris was about to say the same thing in yet another way when . . .

"There!" John said softly, at the same time lowering himself so that only the top of his head and his visual sensors peeked out above the barrier. "Oh, my—"

"What?" Cris interrupted, battling the urge to crawl to John's side and see what he was seeing.

"Two of them — no, three. The lead one is huge, and it has . . . firearms! . . . fastened to its front flanks. The other two look normal."

"Let me see!"

"No — stay down. They've moved behind a building right now, but they're definitely headed in this general direction. I'll take out the one with the weapons, soon as it gets close enough for a good shot. Then we'll handle the other two."

"I didn't come here to hide!" Cris said defiantly.

John wasn't listening. "It's . . . aiming!" he said with amazement. "Aiming this way!"

The largest creature had been picking up readings from its sensors for several minutes, but was not able to pinpoint the source of the signals until it moved away from its protective cover and out into the open. Then it "saw" what it had been seeking, just barely visible above the edge of the roof. It had enough sense not to try hitting such a small target directly. . . .

John couldn't stay hidden any longer. He sprang to his feet, and extended both arms out and down just after the *whump* of the creature's grenade launcher reached his ears.

In the short time it took for John's lasers to lock on target, the grenade shot out in a high trajectory, reached its apex, and came down on the rooftop. In the fraction of a second before John's lasers fired, the projectile hit the roof and exploded about thirty feet away from John and Cris.

The blast didn't hurt them; it didn't even do much damage to the concrete roof. But it did send a slight tremor through the rooftop, just enough to shift John's body ever so slightly and throw off his aim. Before he could correct for the shock wave, John's lasers went off. The twin narrow beams sizzled through the air and missed their target by no more than a foot — but with a laser beam, close doesn't count.

John set himself to re-aim and got off a second shot just as the creature released another grenade. He smiled grimly inside as he saw the beams scorch their way to and through the creature. If he had used that instant to throw himself out of the way, he could have saved himself.

The second grenade came at the rooftop on a straight, ascending line. John picked up its approach in time to throw his body to one side, but not soon enough to avoid it.

The small sphere hit John's upper left torso and exploded. The concussion of the blast threw John backward and to the right, causing him to fall on Cris — who, when the first grenade went off, had started to scramble to his feet. His hands and knees went out from under him at the unexpected impact of John's body on top of his.

"John!" Cris cried, struggling to get out from under him.

"Stay quiet and move slow," John said in a firm but weak voice. "I'm okay."

The remarkable absorption capacity of C-12's outer body covering had confined the explosion damage to the smallest possible area. Cris saw that the pseudoskin over the upper left torso had been mangled and partially blown away. Some of the framework that made up John's cybernetic skeleton was visible, but it didn't look broken or even severely damaged.

"Okay?" Cris said incredulously.

"Well, I'm not *dead*," John replied, trying to keep Cris's spirits up with a bit of humor. "But I can't . . . feel . . . my left leg. I don't think I can move." His voice was even fainter now, just above a gasp, although there was no need for them to whisper any more.

"Stay down," Cris said, crouching beside the other man. "Save your strength. I'll get us out of here." Just then another grenade came plummeting down behind Cris, a few yards from the two of them. Cris heard and felt the explosion, then winced reflexively as a few small chunks of concrete bounced off his back.

He got to his knees, still keeping his body low, grabbed John's body by the ankles, and began to pull him toward the doorway that led to the floor below the roof.

"What . . . ?" John's voice was soft and groggy, sounding like he was either coming out of unconsciousness or lapsing into it. His arms and hands worked, as though he was trying to grab onto something and keep himself from sliding.

"We have to get below," Cris explained as he continued to pull. "Don't talk — just let me do the work." John's only reply to that was a weak groan, but his body stopped resisting, and Cris couldn't tell whether he had fallen unconscious or not.

Just as Cris got himself through the doorway and was about to pull John in behind him, he heard and felt another grenade explode against the rooftop — this one dangerously close to him and John. The thing firing the grenades seemed to be trying to hit the small enclosure on the roof where the doorway was located. Fortunately, they were shielded by the back side of the enclosure — but the next time they might not be so lucky.

Cris got John inside the enclosure, backing down the first few steps of the stairway as he did so. It felt good to be able to stand up again. He reached forward and lifted John's body under the armpits, cringing a bit as his fingers brushed across the damaged area. Cris hoisted C-12 onto his shoulders and walked silently backward down the steps toward the tenth-floor landing. Just as he reached the bottom of the stairway, another grenade blast resounded from above, and the rain of debris that came just afterward told Cris that the doorway had suffered a direct hit. One look skyward confirmed his suspicion; the top of the stairway was clogged with broken concrete and splintered wood.

"Get down!" John said thickly, dreamily. Either the blast had shaken him out of his stupor, or he really was dreaming.

"We are down," Cris answered. "Just relax."

Cris hauled John down one more flight of steps to the ninth floor, not wanting to stay on the upper story in case the roof collapsed. Being careful to stay away from windows, he scouted around until he found a spot where he thought John would be safe. In the time it took him to do this, two more blasts shook the roof. Apparently, Cris thought, the thing figured it had trapped them on the rooftop, and it was going to keep lobbing grenades until it was sure they were dead.

The next thing Cris had to do was even riskier than what he had just been through. Somehow, the creature with the grenades had seemed able to sense where he and John were located. Remembering John's remark about "weapon finders," Cris had deduced that the creature had a way of getting a fix on the radio transmissions that constantly emanated from their bodies — the electronic umbilical cords that enabled the people back at the base to know where they were and what was happening to them.

John was obviously very low on power, and Cris assumed that C-12's transmitter was either out of operation or sending out a signal so weak that it couldn't be picked up. That meant that if Cris turned off his signal, they both would be utterly alone. If something happened to them while he was out of touch and he couldn't re-establish contact, it would be very difficult for the technicians to locate and help them. But it had to be done — no one back at the base could help them right now anyway.

He had to concentrate hard to force his brain to override the inboard computer. He wasn't *supposed* to break radio contact, but the computer *should* let him do it, since it didn't directly threaten his life. . . . There! Cris felt the transmitter shut off. He thought fleetingly about the panic he must be causing back at the base, and he knew he would have some explaining to do, but what he was most concerned about right now was getting back to base and having a chance to explain. . . .

* * *

As Cris had suspected, the receivers monitoring C-12's condition had stopped operating just after John was hit. Losing C-12's signal alarmed the onlookers back at the base, but that reaction was mild compared to what happened when Cris stopped transmitting.

"No!" shrieked Nora in the privacy of her office. She lunged out toward her monitor screen, frantically twisting knobs and checking wires. It was no good — Cris was cut off.

A chill had gone through Nora when John was disabled, but she knew that she and the other personnel at the base could still monitor Cris, and she could tell by his words and his actions that Cris was unhurt and John was merely injured. But now she couldn't see what her son was seeing or hear what he was hearing. She had no way of knowing whether Cris and John were dead or alive.

Fighting off tears and struggling to remain hopeful, but unable to control the trembling of her

307

hands, Nora clutched the armrests of her chair and stared at the featureless screen in front of her. "It's just temporary," she told herself. "Any minute now—"

The sharp rapping on her office door made Nora jump. Her first impulse was that someone had come to tell her Cris was dead. No, she thought. That's impossible. No one knows I'm his mother. . . .

As Nora looked through the one-way viewport on the door, Tony Minelli's face stared back at her. The young man was obviously upset, and he knocked on the door again as she stood there, this time with his fists instead of his knuckles.

Nora took a couple of extra seconds to compose herself before opening the door. "Mister Minelli," she said in a friendly but shaky voice. "What are you doing here?"

"The screens went blank down in the main viewing room," Tony said frantically. "I hoped you'd let me look at yours—"

"It's down too," Nora said as she ushered him inside. "But you're welcome to stay. I could use some company right now," she said, as her eyes started to fill with tears.

"What happened?" Tony asked, oblivious to the fact that Nora was at least as upset as he was. "Are they okay? Cris is the best friend I've ever had, and—"

"I don't know," said Nora in response to both of

Tony's questions. "We've lost Cris's signal, but I couldn't tell if the shutdown was voluntary or not. All we can do is wait—"

"Cris . . . you called him Cris," Tony interrupted. "I've never heard anybody in here use his real name before, except for me." He smiled warmly at the woman standing before him. "He's still a person, you know," Tony continued. "He deserves to be called by his real name."

Nora could hear the love and concern in Tony's voice — love and concern, she supposed, that was no different from what she was feeling. . . . Something inside her broke loose at that moment, and she took a deep breath before replying.

"I couldn't agree with you more, Tony," Nora said. "That's the name I gave him."

"What?"

"Let's sit down," she said softly. "I have something to tell you."

* * *

"John — John! Can you hear me?"

Cris tried to rouse his injured companion as he crouched down beside him. To carry out the rest of his plan, Cris would have to leave his friend here for a while, and he didn't want John to regain consciousness and think he had been deserted.

"Uhhh . . . Cris? You okay?"

Cris was relieved — not only was he conscious,

John seemed to be rational. But he was definitely very, very weak.

"John, I have to leave you here for a while, but I'll be back. Okay?"

"Not yet . . ."

"I have to *go*, John. Do you understand?"

"Wait," John murmured. "Just in case . . . you should know." The middle part of John's statement was drowned out by another explosion, this one followed by a crash on the floor above that indicated part of the roof had caved in.

"What?" Cris asked, trying to remain patient.

"Back at the base . . . someone who cares about you."

"They care about you too, John. I'll get us both out of here." Cris was getting anxious; time was slipping away, and John wasn't making much sense.

"No . . . about *you*," John said, straining to emphasize the word. "Your mother, Cris — your mother is in the base."

"No, my mother—" Cris started to respond, but John cut him off.

"Your *real* mother," he said. "She's the one who asked me to look out for you, and—"

"My mother? My *real* mother? How—" Cris broke off the question, suddenly putting the pieces together in his head. This was what John had been keeping from him; she was the person John had referred to. . . .

"If I don't get back . . . She'll need you." Again, John's words were partially obliterated by another explosion.

"We're *both* going to get back," Cris said, now filled with even more determination to succeed, to survive. He grasped John's right shoulder. "I'll come and get you soon."

"I'm not going anywhere, kid. Good luck."

Cris stood and made his way soundlessly to the outside wall of the building facing the street. He stood with his back to the wall, right next to a window. Then, hoping it wouldn't be the last move he ever made, he whirled and looked out the opening. As soon as he got a good glimpse at the street beneath him, he darted back behind the wall.

The thing with the grenade launchers was crawling haltingly along the opposite side of the roadway. From the way it moved, Cris figured that John's laser blast had done it some damage, but the thing was still aware and dangerous. The weapon on its left side was pointed up, but not directly at the building Cris was in. A *whump* followed shortly thereafter by another blast above him told Cris that the thing was still training its shots on the rooftop — it didn't know that Cris and John had escaped, and it apparently hadn't detected Cris during the moment when he had stood at the window. The other two creatures, apparently not armed, were shuffling along about fifty yards behind their "flagship."

"Okay," Cris said to himself. "Here goes."

He jumped back in front of the window, his arms already extended into attack position. With the speed of thought, his lasers targeted on the bulk below him and fired, and the searing beams took the creature completely by surprise.

The shots cut into the thing's body on either side of its weapon. The launcher fell limp, its muzzle almost touching the pavement — and just as Cris was about to fire again, the weapon spit out a grenade. The projectile blasted a chunk out of the street, sending pieces of ice-covered concrete in all directions. When the debris settled, Cris saw that the blast had also gouged a large hole in the creature's body, and the weapon — now probably useless anyway — had been torn from its flank by the force of the explosion.

"Now you die!" Cris growled. He played his laser beams back and forth, up and down along the creature's motionless body, incinerating it and chopping it into ineffectual, formless pieces at the same time. Even after the thing had ceased showing any signs of life, he fired several more blasts, making small pieces into even smaller ones.

The other two monsters had stopped in their tracks when Cris got off his first shots, and by the time he finished frying the lead creature one of the others had turned slightly so that its left flank was facing the building Cris was in. The thing seemed to have large pores, almost like portholes, in its side. Just as Cris directed his full attention toward the creature, a small object squirted out of one of the holes. It soared upward, out of Cris's view, and an instant later he heard another explosion on the roof.

The second thing — and maybe the other one too — was carrying grenades *inside* itself! But it was still concentrating on the roof, apparently unaware of exactly where Cris's laser fire had come from.

As soon as Cris realized what he was up against, he knew exactly what to do. This is almost too easy, he thought as he allowed himself a second or two to savor what he was about to do. Then he fired.

Instead of playing his lasers up and down, trying to cut the thing into sections, he directed one sweeping shot along the length of the creature's body — cutting right across the openings. As the beams hit the grenades still imbedded inside the thing, the explosive charges went off almost simultaneously. The combined force splattered most of the creature's body all over the street and the adjacent buildings and reduced the rest of the thing to a smoking, pulpy heap.

The third creature was intelligent enough to try getting away — smart enough, but not fast enough. As it turned and presented its flank to Cris's view, he leaned out of the window almost casually and blew it to bits.

"Yahoo!" Cris's cry of exultation split the cold, still air, and he smacked his right fist into his left palm. He pivoted and began trotting back to where he had left John. "I did it!" he yelled as he approached C-12's body. "I did it! They're dead!"

"I heard you the first time," John whispered. "Sounded like quite a blast."

"Oh, yeah," Cris said, happiness and relief washing over him. "I wish you could have been there. . . ."

"Next time, kid. Next time I will be. Now let's get out of here."

Cris got John back over his shoulders and headed for the stairs. He paused before starting his descent, concentrated for a second, and felt his radio transmitter kick back to life.

"This is P-17," he announced proudly. "We're coming home."

Epilogue

Nora Whitaker screamed when her monitor came back on. She leaped from her chair, embraced Tony, and let her tears come — tears of joy that she could shed willingly, happily. From this moment forward, her life would be different — better, so much better. Her past was behind her, her secret was out in the open, and now she could start to live a life free of alcohol, free of guilt . . . free of pain.

Of course, she would still worry every time Cris went outside. But she looked forward to being able to worry openly, honestly — to worry the way a mother has a right to, instead of the way a technician is supposed to. In the midst of a world that was torn and battered, Nora Whitaker was happy beyond her wildest dreams.

Tony Minelli had not been sworn to secrecy after hearing Nora's revelation. In fact, she had made a point of saying that she didn't care who knew about it. So, Tony wasted no time in taking her at her word. Just as Cris and John reached the access bay, Tony burst into the viewing room he had left earlier and told the news to anyone who would listen.

The celebration that was already taking place rose to an even higher peak as the word spread through the chamber. Everyone in the room could appreciate, whether from her standpoint or his, the happiness that both Nora and her son were feeling right now. And in a time when there was precious little to be happy about, they all grabbed this morsel of joy and savored it.

Despite outward appearances, neither John Edwards nor C-12 was in particularly bad shape. The grenade blast had torn away the circuitry that controlled the operation of his left leg, blacked out his radio transmitter, and caused a short circuit that drained away a lot of his primary power. However, all of the damage would be easy to repair. Two days later, John would be chomping at the bit to get back into the battle.

In the weeks and months ahead, C-12 and P-17 would not always be teamed. Both of them had superior intellects, courage, and leadership ability — which, in Cris's case, was recognized by P-17's elevation to lieutenant (the same rank C-12 held) on the day after he had rescued John. Now they were both officers, and at times each of them would be needed to shepherd new recruits just as John had once done for Cris. But they worked together every chance they got, and when they were a team they were, quite simply, the best.

At first, more than anything, Cris Holman wanted to see what his mother looked like. After he had held her, spoken his first words to her, and looked into her eyes, he wanted to know everything about her: Where had she been all these years? How did she get here? Why didn't she *tell* him?

In due time, Cris got all of his answers — and, in turn, he told his mother what had happened to him. He was grateful that he didn't have to relate all of the painful details (thanks to Tony's earlier conversation with his mother), but it comforted him to know that if he wanted to let the memories out, he had a mother who would be glad to listen.

Cris longed for the day when his brain could be put back in his body, so that he could really give his mother back the son she had lost nearly two decades ago. But that desire, strong as it was, did not weaken his resolve to continue what he had started. Cris Holman and P-17 still had a job to do. The world was counting on him.

It was not discouraged, but It was far from satisfied. It was furious — truly enraged — for the first time It could recall.

It knew now that brute force and primitive weaponry would not be sufficient to destroy the machines that the natives of this planet had created. Something stronger was needed, would be brought forth — and if the planet was made uninhabitable in the process, then It would accept that as a necessity. It now wanted more than control — It wanted revenge.

The battle for Earth would not be a short one, and would not be an easy victory. But Its confidence was unshaken.

It would persevere. . . .

THE BATTLE FOR EARTH
CONTINUES IN . . .

Chase Into Space
CYBORG COMMANDO™ Book 2
On sale February 1988

As the Cyborg Commando Force grows in numbers and in skill, the hopes of the beleaguered human race rise as well. The more Cris Holman and his comrades learn about the mysterious invaders, the better they become at beating back the assault. However, as a few members of the Force find out the hard way, this process works in reverse as well — the enemy gets smarter, stronger, and even more determined to lay claim to . . .

The Ultimate Prize
CYBORG COMMANDO™ Book 3
On sale April 1988

Both sides have thrown their entire arsenals against each other, and the furious fight for control of Earth makes so-called conventional warfare seem like a picnic in the park. CCs and invaders alike would sooner die than give up ground to their opponents. The battle can't end in a standoff, because both forces will settle for nothing less than the annihilation of the other. One side will win . . . but which one?